Destination Prairie

Two Years to a Lifetime:
A Young Highlander's Journey in her New Land

CATHIE BARTLETT

BAYEUX ARTS
DIGITAL-TRADITIONAL PUBLISHING

DESTINATION PRAIRIE:

Publication: September 2019

Published in Canada by
Bayeux Arts Digital – Traditional Publishing
2403, 510 6th Avenue, S.E.
Calgary, Canada T2G 1L7

www.bayeux.com

Book design by Lumina Datamatics
Cover image, 1921 *Canada West* Magazine cover. Courtesy, Glenbow archives,
Calgary, Canada.

Library and Archives Canada Cataloguing in Publication

Title: Destination prairie : two years to a lifetime : a young highlander's journey in
her new land
    / Cathie Bartlett.
Names: Bartlett, Cathie, author.
Identifiers: Canadiana (print) 20190153571 | Canadiana (ebook) 2019015358X |
ISBN 9781988440392
    (softcover) | ISBN 9781988440408 (HTML)
Classification: LCC PS8603.A7836 D47 2019 | DDC C813/.6—dc23

The ongoing publishing activities of Bayeux Arts Digital – Traditional
Publishing under its varied imprints are supported by the Canada Council
for the Arts, the Government of Alberta, Alberta Multimedia Development
Fund, and the Government of Canada through the Book Publishing Industry
Development Program.

Canada Council
for the Arts

Conseil des Arts
du Canada

Alberta Culture

LIVRES CANADA BOOKS

Canada
Government of Canada through
the Canada Book Fund

Printed in Canada

For my beloved daughter Leah

Southeastern Alberta
March 1922

Chapter One

Snow...thick, heavy snow, masses of it, pelting the window in one determined thud after another, pulling me out of the bottomless sleep I had lapsed into after boarding the train in Medicine Hat only an hour before. "So that's what it is," I murmured after taking a blurred glance outside and realizing there was a blizzard happening. Where on earth are we? I wondered as I pressed my face against the glass and peered into the troubled night sky. All that snow, the wind is whipping it into a blinding rage and it's making me feel colder than I already am. I can't make out a thing, maybe if the lights were a bit dimmer, I thought, raising my right hand to my forehead to block the glare of the lanterns perched high inside the coach.

But that didn't help. So I settled down into my seat, hoping to escape back into sleep, wishing this wretched journey would end. As I tried to make myself comfortable I looked toward the window and immediately wished I hadn't; I didn't need to see my reflection just then, my hair hanging in limp strands, dark semi-circles underlining my eyes and my face paler than ever. Not even a week in the new country and look what it has done to me, I thought.

"What's that, miss?" a cheerful male voice asked, startling me out of my thoughts. I jerked around to see who was talking to me, knocking my purse onto the floor in the process.

"Here, I'll get that for you," the same voice said, and there bending over to retrieve my bag was the conductor who had helped me onto the train.

"Oh, oh thank you. That's so nice of you," I told him.

"Not at all," he replied, smiling at me. "Can I do anything else for you?" he asked as he stepped back into the aisle.

"Yes, can you tell me where we are? It's so dark out there I cannot see a thing."

"About five miles from Diamond Coulee. We'll just have to sit and wait until the weather lets up a bit. That shouldn't be too long, I believe the storm is starting to lift. Let me know if you need any more help," he said as he started down the aisle.

"Aye, I will, and thank you," I told him. Since I was almost at my destination I gave up trying to get more sleep, deciding instead to read the newspaper a departing passenger had left on the seat across from me. As I scanned the front page I heard a young boy across the aisle giggle and tell his mother, "She has a strange way of talking."

"Shush, Gregory, have you no manners at all. That's not polite," his mother said sternly, then turned to me and smiled. "Pardon my son's impertinence. He hasn't heard too many people from Scotland. It *is* Scotland you're from, isn't it?"

"Aye, I mean, yes, it is," I replied, setting off another burst from the boy.

"Gregory, that will be enough from you, do you hear? And whereabouts in Scotland, if I may ask?"

"Inverness, up in the Highlands," I answered.

"And what brings you so far? Are you joining your parents?"

"Not quite. My brother is meeting me at Diamond Coulee. He teaches near there."

"And are you going to teach as well?" she asked.

"No, I'm going to look after his children."

"Ah, his wife needs some help, does she?"

"As a matter of fact his wife passed away last summer. He has two little girls and it's been hard for him to manage the house and keep teaching. The neighbours have been kind and they help when they can but…"

"But he needs someone in charge,' the woman responded. "He's lucky to have you willing to come all this way." A tiny frown puckered her eyebrows. "Do you know, come to think of it, I recall your brother and his dear wife. Such a pretty young woman, always had a smile for me when I saw her at church or the store. My husband and I live on a farm a few miles out of Diamond Coulee, that's how we knew of them. What a tragedy when your sister-in-law, Elizabeth, wasn't that her name? when Elizabeth passed away, and the baby boy taken as well. We all felt so badly. I'm glad you're here to help, dear. I'll be looking for you next time I'm in the village. Now Gregory, let's gather up our things. The train sounds like it might get going at last, and we want to be ready when we get to Diamond Coulee. You know your father does not like to be kept waiting. My name is Mrs. Taylor, Mary Taylor, and you are…?" she asked as she leaned across her seat to collect her son's scarf and hat. "Your last name must be Sinclair; your brother is Robert Sinclair, is he not?"

"Yes he is, and my name is Grace Sinclair," I managed to edge in. "It was nice meeting you," I lied, happy to see the nosy woman and her rude son go away, relieved I didn't have to explain my circumstances further. Hardly anyone else's business, especially someone I met five minutes ago; is everyone else I run into going to interrogate me like that, I wondered as I gathered up my own things and moved a few seats closer to the exit, where I plunked myself down and looked out into the now calmer darkness. I will be so glad when this is over, I sighed to myself. A week on the boat and another five days on the train, so tiring and so far from Inverness....imagine, it wasn't so long ago that I was certain I was going to live my entire life there; how things can change, I mused, letting my mind drift over the collage of events that steered me to this windswept corner of Alberta.

Chapter Two

It started when Father died five years ago. When he went so did my hopes of going to teacher's college in Edinburgh when I finished at the collegiate. Mother was left with few means and much of what little she had went towards helping Robert take teacher training after he returned from the Great War with an injured leg. He had a family of his own to support; he had married his sweetheart Elizabeth when he was home on leave partway through the war and their first child, Alice, was born the summer after the fighting ended. Not that Mother's sacrifice hadn't brought the return she hoped for; jobs were hard to come by for returned veterans, especially injured veterans. Even so, the young family was struggling. Then one day Robert spied a notice in *The Scotsman* about postings for teachers in the Canadian west.

How excited Robert was when he brought Elizabeth and Alice over for tea a few days later. "They're begging for teachers in Alberta. I could teach in a country school for a few years; the school board would provide a house for us, and after that I could move on to a school in the city, Calgary or Edmonton maybe. I could be a headmaster, principals they call them there, years before I could even hope to advance here," he said, as the six of us – our brother Simon was home from Aberdeen where he was apprenticing as a printer – gathered around the kitchen table. "I have my application filled out and ready to send off tomorrow morning."

I remember the uneasy silence that followed Robert's announcement. It wasn't as if Canada was unknown to us, nor Alberta for that matter. We all knew how our late Grandfather Sinclair had struck out from his birthplace on one of the rugged Orkney Isles after signing up with the Hudson's Bay Company when he was twenty-three. He wound up in surroundings almost as remote as those he left, Fort Edmonton, an HBC post on the banks of the North Saskatchewan River. He was posted there for five years, building York boats that were used to carry furs and trader goods along the inland waterways of the company's extensive territory. From the sparse details he gave up on those rare occasions when he spoke of his time away, we gathered he had liked his time in Fort Edmonton well enough. The farm he grew up on had little to offer him being as he was the fourth son in a family of ten children. He'd always had a bent for wood-working and the HBC contract offered steady employment, something else that was in short supply around Orkney. When his term with HBC was done he had enough money saved to establish himself 'down south' in the Highlands, where he found work at a fishmonger's, married and helped our sweet Granny raise three sons and a daughter.

"I can understand why you want to do this," Mother said. "It's just that Canada is so far away, and with your father gone…" she said, her voice trailing off. A moment or two later she spoke up again, firmly this time. "This is fine, Robert, you have your own family to think of and we won't stand in your way."

Robert was at the Immigration Office the next day and it wasn't long before we were waving him off again, only this time he wasn't in uniform and he wasn't alone. I missed Elizabeth and little Alice so much. Frankly, I had never been close to either of my brothers when I was growing up – to Robert and Simon I was too young to bother with and a girl besides – but Elizabeth was like the sister I never had. After she and Robert married, she moved into his room to await his return from the front. We spent a lot of time together, stitching and reading in the evenings after the washing up was done and I had finished my schoolwork. Saturday afternoons we'd go to the shops and the public library and every Sunday morning to church with Mother. Of course after Robert came back I didn't see much of Elizabeth during the week but Saturdays I was always welcome at their place for a cup of tea and a visit, and when Alice came along we often took her out in her pram.

I don't know who was sadder – Mother or I – when Robert took his family away to Canada. For the longest time we kept the door to Robert's old room closed and we felt so isolated, as if the distance from Inverness and the faraway corner of Alberta that claimed them had settled between the two of us. Most evenings Mother sat in the kitchen, knitting or sewing, while I stayed upstairs in my room to finish my schoolwork or read. I started spending more time with Phoebe, a girl in my class I had chummed with since primary school, going to the library and window shopping on the high street. We became close friends. Yet I missed Elizabeth and Alice a lot, and every afternoon when I came home from school the first thing I did was check to see what the postman had brought.

At first we didn't hear all that often from our absent family. "Imagine they are busy settling in," Mother would say with a sigh as another day passed without a letter from Canada. Finally, Robert wrote, telling of another child on the way, and a few months later announcing Louisa's arrival. A while after that, Elizabeth took over as correspondent. We so enjoyed her lengthy letters detailing their new life: the rough one-room school where Robert taught and the solitary ride by horse-drawn buggy or sleigh to get there; the treeless stretches of land-scape that seemed to go on forever; the dramatic seasons with the intense heat in summer and fearsome cold in winter... each letter savoured, read and re-read before being tucked away in the desk in the parlour.

Not long after Louisa was born Elizabeth wrote she was expecting another baby, due early that fall. "Rather soon," Mother said, looking a little worried. "I hope it isn't too much for her." Weeks passed by with nothing more from Elizabeth, then finally I came home from school one damp afternoon to find an envelope postmarked Diamond Coulee lying on the floor of the front landing. Mother must have been so busy in the kitchen she didn't hear the mail slot drop, I thought, as I picked up the envelope, surprised to see my brother's handwriting on it.

"More news of our wee ones, from Robert this time," I said as I walked into the kitchen and handed the letter to Mother. "So it is. Perhaps Elizabeth was too tired to write. Fetch the letter-opener would you, Grace?" That done, Mother slit the envelope and pulled out a single sheet of paper folded haphazardly in half once and then again. "Let's see what Robert has to say." She had barely started reading when a look of total disbelief overtook her face. "Oh no, oh no, it cannot be," she said, her voice breaking, her hands shaking as she set the letter down.

"What is it, Mum? What is wrong?" I asked.

"The... the... the baby came early, a boy. He... he died at birth, and Elizabeth soon after," she said, her voice yielding to a huge sob as she put her hands to her face and wept. "What are we to do?" she moaned. I had no answer but even if I had thought of anything to say I had such a lump in my throat I could not have forced the words out. I took Mother's arm and guided her towards the kitchen table, pulling out a chair for her and another one for myself. I put my arm around my mother's shoulder, and there we remained, staring silently at the table as the afternoon gave way to evening, the fading light eventually nudging us out of our daze to put together a sketchy meal that neither of us wanted to eat.

There were more days like that, days when even thinking, let alone saying or doing anything, was exhausting. Will we ever get used to this? I asked myself as I trudged home one fall afternoon. Who said time heals all things? First Father, now Elizabeth and the little one – are we a marked house? Everywhere I went images of Elizabeth flashed before me: stopping in at the newsagent for the paper and a few sweets; showing me a new stitch as we took up our needlework for another evening; slipping me a chocolate as we sat in the cinema waiting for the Saturday matinee to start; doodling on the back of the program at church on Sunday morning; holding Alice up to the train window and waving good-bye...

"Grace, would you come here please?" my mother called upstairs one grey Sunday afternoon in November. It had been a boring day; my schoolwork was done, I couldn't call on Phoebe because she was busy with her grandmother who was visiting from Edinburgh and it was too cold to go out for a walk. Glad for something to do, I tossed aside the book I had been trying to get interested in and hustled down to the kitchen, taking the stairs two at a time.

"Slow down, girl, you'll hurt yourself one of these days," my mother scolded as I charged through the kitchen door.

"Shall I set the table for tea, Mum?" I asked, heading straight to the sideboard to get the dishes and cutlery.

"Would you leave that be, dear, that's not why I asked you here. Please sit down. I've got something to discuss with you," my mother said, wiping her forehead with her apron as she stirred the lamb stew simmering on the range.

She was so fidgety, I remembered afterwards. Always the one who knew what she was going to say and do, and quick about it, and here Mum was so uneasy, fumbling with the lid as if she didn't know how to put it on the pot and taking all kinds of time to sit down at the table herself.

"It's about your brother and his situation," Mum started out, hesitating, unsure it seemed about what to say next. Then the words came out in a rush, about Robert needing someone to look after the children and keep up the house; that he could not depend on the neighbours forever nor could he afford to hire a housekeeper even if he could find someone suitable.

"Most want to look after a widower or be a companion to an older woman; they are not wanting to chase after two wee ones on top of everything else there is to do in running a house. I don't want to see you go far away, you as well, after Robert, especially after losing your father and Simon's work taking him to Aberdeen…. It will be so quiet here I don't know how I will bear it. It's just there is not much for you here, and I can't keep you forever. With Robert you would have your lodging and a decent place at that, and a bit of pocket money and you would be seeing a new land…," Mum said, her voice dropping as she finished her spiel. Silence followed for a moment, swiftly broken as I absorbed what my mother had just proposed.

"Do you mean I would *live* in Canada?" I asked. "What are you thinking, I've never been there and you want me to pack up and leave just like that, to raise a little one I have not seen for three years and another I have yet to meet, and to keep house for a brother I hardly know anymore? I must say this is a lot you are expecting of me! This is preposterous! I want to be a teacher, at a school in the Highlands, where I belong, not a cook and nanny in some godforsaken place half the world away," I fumed.

"You can't make me do this; I won't!" I declared as I pushed my chair aside, stood up and marched towards the kitchen door.

"Grace Kathleen Sinclair, where do you think you are going?" Mother called out.

"Back to my room, that's where!"

"Come back here and sit down. We are not finished this discussion," Mother replied. Fists clenched, eyes flashing, I returned to the table and sat down, shoving the chair back with a determined thrust. "Here, I'll get us a cup of tea," she said.

"I don't want any tea."

"Well I do," Mum responded, filling the kettle and putting it on the stove. "And I'll thank you to stop scowling at me, young lady." Nothing more was said as the tea was made and two cups and saucers placed on the table.

"Try to understand, Grace," Mother said as she poured the tea. "There is more opportunity for a family in Canada. Robert is limited as to what work he can do with his leg hurt and he does not want to give up his teaching position. Times have been hard out his way but things are predicted to improve in the school district, and with more settlers going out to farm there will be more schools and bigger ones. Robert stands to do well, and as for you, what is there to occupy you here? You know full well I can't afford to send you on in school and there are not many suitable jobs in the shops. If you stay here you probably would have to go into service or something."

"So I'm to cross the sea and go into service for my brother, am I?"

"You would be going to help your brother and his children. They need you, can't you understand that?" Mother asked.

"Oh I understand," I said. "I know they need help but I still think this is asking a lot of me, can *you* not understand that? Robert chose to go to Canada, I did not."

My mother sighed and got up to stir the stew. "Please set the table now Grace. We will talk about this another day. I am going down to the cold room to get a few things and I expect to find you in a more civil frame of mind when I come back."

"As if we have anything more to discuss," I muttered after my mother left the room. "Nursemaid in Canada indeed."

The matter hung between us for the next few days, unspoken, ending conversations before they began, shrinking the space in the small row house to the point I avoided being in the same room with my mother as much as possible, going straight to my room when I came in after school and heading back upstairs as soon as the evening meal was consumed and the washing up done. Yet there was no escaping the issue. Canada, *not* going to Canada, was all I could think of and all I talked about with Phoebe. "Tell your mum it's your life,' Phoebe suggested during one of our discussions. "Ask her how she would like to leave everything and everyone she knows."

And so it went, until the Saturday after the whole matter arose. Odd how abruptly my thoughts changed, I mused a few months later as I packed my trunk. Maybe I knew all along that Mum was right, that going on in school was out of the question and jobs were scarce so, really, what was I going to do. And of course Robert needed me, I knew that. But it was stopping in at the newsagent's on the way home from Phoebe's house that Saturday afternoon that decided me, when I saw Jenny the shop girl behind the counter as usual and the women from the neighbourhood chatting as they picked up their newspapers before heading home to make evening tea as they always did. Then I glanced down at the newspaper I was about to buy and there on the front page was an article about Canada, what it was about escapes me now, but seeing mention of the country triggered something in me. Here I had the chance to go somewhere else and do something different and that could be interesting, exciting even. I could go to Alberta for a while, a year or two; yes, two years, until the little ones were older and Robert more settled in his career.

At any rate, I surprised myself and startled a few others in the bargain. "I'll go, but only on condition I can come back in two years, that's long enough to get Robert and the girls on their feet," I told Mother as we walked home from church the next day.

"Fair enough, dear," Mother answered, sounding as if she wasn't sure whether to be happy or sad. "I am sure Robert will agree. I'll write to him tonight. He will be so relieved."

"So you really are going to Canada? You can't be serious!" Phoebe exclaimed as she rocked her sister's new baby and tried to keep an eye on her two nephews running about the kitchen. "James, put that tea towel back on the rack. It is for drying dishes, not for tripping your brother. Put it back I say, put it back right now. Shush, wee one, don't mind the racket," she cooed to the baby. "Here, let's put you on my shoulder and see how you like that," she told the tightly-wrapped bundle.

Halfway through the procedure she looked across the table at me. "What will I do without you?" Phoebe blurted, her face crumpling. "Canada is so far away. Will I ever see you again?"

"Oh Phoebe, it's not forever," I said, fumbling in my pocket for my handkerchief. "I expect to be back in a few years. I told Mum I would go only if I could return in two years if I want and I am sure that is what I will want."

Phoebe looked up from her baby niece. "But I'll miss you so much," she wailed, bursting into tears.

Once word was out, I found myself quite the person of interest in the neighbourhood. The clerk at the butcher shop called me by name – that had never happened before – and asked about the impending move, sounding a touch wistful as she did. People who had only nodded to me at church now came up to me after the service each week to ask how the plans for Canada were coming along, and whenever I bumped into a former classmate a progress report was demanded before I could proceed on my way.

A month or so after Christmas Robert sent an envelope thick with a bank money order for my transportation and instructions about papers from the Immigration Office. In short order the forms were handled, my passage arranged, my steamer trunk packed and a farewell tea held in the church parlour. My last night at home, Phoebe came over with a good-bye gift, a box of stationary "so you'll have no excuse not to write to me.... I would have put stamps on the envelopes but you have to use stamps from over there, not here."

"Of course I'll write to you, and I've got something for you," I told her, holding out the cushion I started stitching for her the day after I consented to go to Canada. "They're asters, your birth flower," I said, pointing to the lilac and mauve blossoms I had embroidered across the front of the pillow.

Next morning it was my turn to start out for Canada, with Mum and Phoebe waving good-bye from the platform. "And here I am," I murmured, trying for the hundredth time at least to push aside the unsettled feeling that descended as the train chugged out of Inverness.

"Go away, go away," I whispered, glancing outside, noticing that thick clouds the colour of grey soot still cluttered the sky but the snow had stopped. Right then the train started up with a mighty shudder, billowing steam as it resumed its determined push along the track. My goodness, maybe we'll get there tonight after all, I thought as the pace quickened. Bored, I reached for the newspaper and skimmed the pages, trying to read as the train clacked along but finally the swaying motion got the best of me and I gave up, put the paper down, stretched out a bit and closed my eyes. Oh no, what now, I groaned to myself a brief while later as the train started slowing down.

"Next stop Diamond Coulee," the conductor called out.

Chapter Three

Diamond Coulee, Alberta
March 18, 1922

Dear Phoebe,

I promised you I would write as soon as I could and here I am. I have not sat down for more than two minutes at a time since I arrived in Diamond Coulee a week ago. It took forever to get here – at times I wondered if I ever would. A huge snowstorm reared up on the last part of the journey, delaying my arrival. Robert wrapped me in two blankets and put a hot water bottle underneath my feet but it was still dreadfully cold on the way to his house. The next morning was almost as cold but by the afternoon the weather turned around completely, with the sun melting the snow and puddles everywhere – a chinook it is called. They happen a lot here I am told.

Now we are in the midst of yet another storm. We have had at least ten inches of snow since last night and still it is falling. I am sitting at the kitchen table and when I look out it seems as if granules of sugar are coming down from the sky. The particles are minute yet they accumulate readily enough. Robert had to push with all his might to open the back door this morning to get out to the stable. There are icicles like daggers hanging from the eaves and the windows are frosted over in places. The few times I have been outside – to feed the chickens and shake out mats – the chill air makes me hustle inside before it catches me out.

I have managed to unpack my clothes and establish myself in the corner of the wee attic room that I share with the girls. Actually, the whole house – teacherage as it is known – is small. It is mostly on one floor, with a narrow entryway leading to the parlour off to one side and the larger bedroom off to the other side. The kitchen is across the back of the house, with a back porch used mainly for storage. As you go from the front entrance to the kitchen you pass a short staircase that takes you up to the attic. When Robert took me up there I could not believe this tiny room was all I had and I don't even have it to myself. But I am getting used to it.

I must say I have my work cut out for me. There is much to do in the way of housecleaning; however, my first concern is getting to know Alice and Louisa. For the first while they seemed not to know what to think of me but yesterday and today they have agreed to sit next to me while I read to them and Alice even called me 'Auntie Grace' this morning.

Alice was still a baby when you last saw her. Now she is three years old; a sturdy girl with brown hair and eyes, much like her dear mother although she bears some resemblance to my side of the house. Robert took us to Medicine Hat for supplies yesterday and a few people in the shops thought she was my own daughter. What a thought – I was only fourteen when she was born. She is a lively lass, showing a bit of a stubborn streak but overall she is fairly easygoing. Louisa is not quite two years old and just starting to talk. She looks much like her sister although her hair is a bit fairer. The two get along well most of the time, although every now and then one of their toys suddenly becomes precious and there is a little set-to but they soon make amends.

The days are very busy. I am up early to get breakfast as Robert has to be off early to get to the school house, which is three miles away. He has to light the stove and haul water for the cooler, sweep the floor and write lessons on the board before his pupils arrive. He is usually away before the little ones are up. After I get them breakfast there is the washing up, sweeping and dusting to do. I play with Alice and Louisa for a bit before lunch. When they are napping I can do some more tidying up. Once they are awake the house is so much livelier and it's an effort to get much of anything done.

I so look forward to warmer weather when I can take the girls for a walk in the village. There is not much here to be sure, a general store with a wicket and counter at one end that passes for a post office, two churches and a little restaurant run by a Chinese man. The farm folk gather at one or the other place when they come into the village for supplies. I don't get out much and I don't know anyone to stop and visit with at the store so it's just as well that I am busy with the girls and the house to keep up. How I wish there was someone else to talk to! I miss you very much, Phoebe, and I will be watching for a letter from you so please hurry with news of home as I am most anxious to hear it.

Your dear friend,
Grace

Chapter Four

Diamond Coulee, Alberta,
April 30, 1922

Dear Phoebe,

Your letter arrived last week. How lovely to hear from you. So you are to be an aunt once more – your sister will have her hands full (and so will you) with another wee one so soon after the last.

The weather is much better than last time I wrote to you. The snow is gone and the grass is starting to turn green. Robert says it will be a while before the leaves come out on the trees; what few trees there are around here, that is. This is an odd area I must say, with rolling fields that drop off sharply now and then into steep valleys, coulees as they are called, which is where you are more likely to find whatever trees are there may be – a bit of unpredictability that I like amongst the open stretches of country and the endless sky. So very different from home; however, I am getting used to it.

This morning I took Alice and Louisa out for a walk to the main street to the general store. The girls ran about so fast I could barely keep up with them. They were as eager to stretch their legs and go outside as I was, after being inside so much the last while. I recognized a few people at the store from Easter service at church a few weeks ago, and then the nicest thing happened. A woman I met on the train coming here, a Mrs. Taylor, approached me and greeted me by name, asking me how I was getting along in my new home. How nice to have someone recognize me.

I have not met many people yet since arriving here, which makes your letters all the more welcome. I hear there will be a church picnic in early June and the school district holds a social later in June for all the staff and their families before the school year ends. I am looking forward to both gatherings.

There is not much new to tell you apart from the improved weather. The countryside is at a standstill until the fields dry up and another farming season begins. When that happens Robert will have fewer students attending school as the older children stay home to help. He is thinking of taking a farm job this summer to make ends meet but of course he cannot do too much heavy work.

Do you know what you will do next year? Wouldn't it be lovely if your sister and her husband took a notion to move to Canada and you could come with them? That is wishful thinking I know! At least I am not the only newcomer around here; Alberta is full of people from all over. I am just thankful I do not have to learn a new language, although I do have trouble understanding some of the expressions I hear and read, and sometimes the store owner doesn't catch what I'm saying and asks me to repeat what I'm asking for.

I must get the evening meal started. The girls are sound asleep after all the fresh air this morning. Please give my best to your parents and your sister. I hope that you are well, dear friend, and that I will hear from you again soon.

Love,
Grace

I folded the letter and set it down on the table, then started to address the envelope but didn't get far before I stopped writing, folded my arms and put my head down on the table. "I am *so* tired,

I haven't slept through the night all week," I sighed to myself. For three nights running Alice had woken up in the midst of a nightmare. Each time it happened I wrapped her in a blanket and rocked her on my knee until she nodded off and then it was a while before I could get back to sleep. Other times it was the wind rattling the windows that awakened me, a sound I had come to despise, and one night a blizzard came up out of nowhere it seemed, a tantrum of wind and snow that scared the girls into bed with me. And oh, how bored I get, the dullness, the routine – cooking, washing up, laundry, looking after the children, day after day; when we do get out it's always the same places – down the boardwalk to the general store, church; no bridge across the river to the city centre like at home, no library or market close by, the nearest place of any size is Medicine Hat and we have been there once and likely there will be six moons in the sky before we are back there.

I sighed again. Seven weeks in and I have had more than my fill of this place. Everyone at home thought this was such a big adventure, going off to a new country so far away, if only they knew… Tears sprang from my eyes and I gave in to the groundswell of discontent lurking in my heart and wept… but not for long. I can't let the girls see me like this, and I have things to do before Robert is home, I told myself firmly.

I stood up and looked at the clock above the kitchen sink. Yes, I do need to get going at supper and then I think I will see if the parlour needs some attention. I haven't cleaned in there at all except for sweeping the floor once or twice. I can get the letter to Phoebe ready for tomorrow's post later on. I wiped my face with my apron and shoved the letter and partly addressed envelope underneath the bread box off to the side of the sink. Let me see, an apple spice cake would go well with the stoved chicken for tonight's supper, I thought, reaching for the Purity cookbook on the shelf beneath the cupboards and turning to the cakes section, recalling how Robert had made a point of showing me that particular cookbook when he was showing me around the house. "One of the neighbour women brought it over a few days after we arrived. Elizabeth made many fine dishes from it," he had said, his voice catching ever so slightly.

I set to work creaming the shortening and sugar, then measured out the flour and rooted around one of the cupboards for the nutmeg, allspice and cinnamon, sugar and salt. I hope we still have some raisins, I thought, as I added the milk and applesauce alternately with the dry ingredients to the shortening and sugar mixture. Now for the raisins, where are they. A brief search through the same cupboard followed. Aha, there they are, hiding behind the rolled oats. I rinsed raisins and dropped them into the mixing bowl, stirred everything well one last time and poured the cake batter into the greased and floured square pan waiting on the counter. A quick smoothing over with a dinner knife and the cake went straight into the oven.

Now for the parlour, I thought, wiping my hands on my apron as I crossed the kitchen and headed across the hallway. As it turned out there was quite a bit of dusting and straightening to do, not that I was surprised, given that my brother spent most of his evenings there. Each night after supper Robert would tip back his chair after he finished his tea, say he had to plan the next day's lessons, catch up on his marking, fill out attendance reports for the school district or get ready for the next visit from the inspector. He'd head off to the parlour where he stayed until he turned in for the night. There was no doubting he had plenty to do, from the looks of the bulging leather satchel he loaded into the buggy every morning along with the lunch I packed for him, and sure enough he was usually poring over some document or other or writing energetically when I took the girls in to say goodnight to their father.

Let's see, what can I tidy up here, I wondered, glancing at Robert's desk, heaped with papers and books. I think it best be left alone; I'll just dust off the lampshade and the paperweight. I did just that, and then my eyes dropped to the wedding picture parked underneath the lamp. "I remember that day so well," I whispered as I gently ran the dust cloth over the black and white image and the heavy silver frame encasing it. "I was so happy you were part of our family. Robert misses you and so do I."

Next I turned my attention to the far side of the room that was taken up with a bookcase and a makeshift sewing corner. After dusting off the sewing machine and bench, I knelt down to pick up a stack of patterns piled up on the floor beside the bench. I can put these on top of the bookcase, I figured. Now what in heaven's name is this? I asked myself as I spied a rumpled cloth object behind the sewing machine. Why it looks like a bag of some sort, I thought as I tugged my find under the treadle and up onto the bench. Indeed, it was a bag. I pried the drawstrings open for a look at the contents which turned out to be several pieces of fabric, a spool of thread and a needle case, a pair of scissors and some brightly coloured embroidery floss. I wonder what this was going to be, I pondered, spreading the bits of fabric out across the floor. Why it's a wee smocked dress; Elizabeth must have started it for Alice, I thought, smiling as I gazed at the half-done garment. I could finish it, although it likely will be Louisa who wears it. I can work on it now. With that I bundled up my discovery and returned to the kitchen where I spread my new project on the table, took up a needle and began filling in the row of stitches my sister-in-law had begun the year before.

I have missed this, I thought, as I pushed the needle in and out, pulling the floss from dot to dot across the bodice of the dress. Fancywork, Grandmother Sinclair called it when she introduced me to stitching, so pleased she was that her granddaughter shared the same bent for needlework. More often than not Sunday afternoons in the winter found the two of us sitting by the fire in Grandmother's parlour, embroidering flowers and butterflies on pillowcases and tea cloths. So nice to have had that time together, before the stroke and Grandmother went into the nursing home, I mused as I smoothed the fabric and guided the needle amongst the gathers. After working a few rows of lilac and deep rose stitches in the shirred pale pink cotton, I held the bodice up. A satisfying feeling such as I had not felt since leaving home spread over me. A few more afternoons and I will be done, I thought, smiling as I shoved the dress back into the bag and crossed the kitchen to take the fragrant smelling cake from the oven. I can't wait to get back at it, I thought as I put out some biscuits and milk for Alice and Louisa, just up from their nap, and set about making the rest of the evening meal.

As it turned out the dress was more than a few afternoons' work, a good number more, not that I minded. I kept at my new-found task, snatching moments here and there when the children were playing or sleeping to ply the needle and thread in and out of the puckered fabric. Indeed, I was disappointed more than anything else when I worked the last rows of rope and stem stitches across the bodice and around the puff sleeves. I must find another bit of stitching to do, I thought as I sewed the little rounded collar in place after assembling the rest of the garment. There, it's all done, and I do like it.

Chapter Five

And so did others.

"Quite a fetching dress your little one is wearing, Mr. Sinclair," said Mrs. Anderson, the principal's wife, who was standing next to Robert at the end of the field watching the races at the year-end picnic, a rare day when their school district mingled with neighbouring districts for something other than academic pursuits. "Did your mother send it over?"

"No, my sister Grace finished it. Actually my wife started it. Grace came across it one day and took up where Elizabeth left off," Robert replied, his voice hurrying to get the explanation out of the way.

"And she did a fine job of it," Mrs. Anderson said. "Grace is liking Canada I hope."

"Oh yes," Robert said.

"She's quite the cook, I must say. The rhubarb tart she brought didn't last long. My lemon squares were always the favourite but not this year," she said, a faint laugh rounding out her remark. "Oh and here's the young lady herself," she said as I approached hand-in-hand with Alice and Louisa. "Well, I see my husband is about to launch the potato sack race. I should go over and see if he needs a hand. Don't forget to take your plate home, Grace," she said, nodding in the direction of the nearly bare table that only an hour or two before was laden with pastries, puddings and other home-baked treats. "Nice to see you all of you."

"And you, Mrs. Anderson," Robert said. "And *you*," he murmured to me once the older woman was out of earshot. "I never thought I would rue your good cooking but I guess there is a first time for everything. Your dessert disappeared into thin air while hers went almost unnoticed. You've put her nose out of joint, you have. I don't know if it's good for my future with the district but it was amusing nonetheless," he said with a laugh, turning his attention to his daughters who had found a few other youngsters to play with. After a few moments Robert looked up and gazed over the picnic grounds, his face once again breaking into a smile as he waved to a man and woman heading their way.

"William, how are you?" Robert called out, then lowering his voice to tell Grace: "It's William Brown from the school at Seven Persons, with his cousin Rosemary. I believe she teaches at Irvine."

"Hello, William, it's been a while," he said as the pair neared.

"Yes, it has been some time," the other man said. "That meeting in Medicine Hat when the bigwigs from the department came down from Edmonton to speak to us, I believe that was the last time I saw you. It's been a busy year for me; quite a large class. You remember my cousin Rosemary Smythe from Irvine School?"

"Yes, you introduced us at last year's wind-up. Nice to see you again, Miss Smythe. How was your year at Irvine?"

"Just fine, Mr. Sinclair, and how did you do at Diamond Coulee? I hear it was a good-sized class."

"Indeed it was, and likely to be bigger next year. My goodness, I've neglected to introduce you to my sister Grace, who came over from Inverness this past March to help with my daughters and keep house, and a fine job she is doing of both."

"Nice to meet you, Grace," the young woman said, nodding in my direction. "How are you liking Canada so far?"

"Well enough, especially now that the warmer weather is here," I replied.

"Ah but wait until our summer heat drops down on us. I hope it is not too warm for you then. You won't want to do much baking then and I am sure your brother will regret that. Your rhubarb tart was delicious. Did the rhubarb come from your own garden?"

"Thank you very much, and yes, it is from our own yard," I said. A legacy from a previous tenant at the teacherage was what it was.

One afternoon a few months before, when the children were so restless they could not sit still for more than a minute, I decided a walk outside would do all of us some good, even if it was rather chilly and clouds were scurrying across the sky. So I bundled the girls up and off we headed to the store. Once inside the building, I set about making good on my promise of a candy for each of them. While the girls surveyed the row of glass jars on the confectionary shelf, deciding which sweet would be best, I overheard a few women from the village talking about what plants they would be setting out come spring. That bit of garden chat reminded me of seeing some garden tools in the shed while putting the children's sled away one afternoon. As I paid for the candies the girls had picked out I made a mental note to check the yard out sometime soon. At nap time a few days later I went out to the back yard. By then the snow was gone and yes, there was a patch of exposed ground that had once been a garden, judging from the wooden stakes and bits of string and wire mesh here and there. As I looked over the waterlogged soil, planning what I could plant and where, I came across a dark green layer of what appeared to be dead leaves and underneath that... Can it be? I wondered, holding my breath as I poked at the winter-ravaged plant, pulling off the lifeless growth to expose a clump of baby pink stalks crowned by tightly furled leaves of the palest green. Rhubarb, just like Grandma Sinclair had in her back yard.

"I was pleased to see it grows so well here," I said, swiftly bringing myself back to the present. "My grandmother had a large rhubarb patch in her garden back home. She gave what she couldn't use to my mother." Feeling a bit awkward, I told the group I'd best see what Alice and Louisa were up to. "Nice meeting you, Miss Smythe and Mr. Brown. Robert, we should be getting home soon. The girls will be tired after running about all afternoon in the sun."

Yet, an hour later I was still sitting with the girls under the trees by the creek while off in the distance my brother and his colleagues sat at the picnic table, deep in conversation. Eventually the group disbanded and Robert made his way over to collect us for the ride home. All the way he was quieter than usual, ignoring the girls as they chattered away about the day's events. Once home, he said he would not be wanting any supper; he had had plenty to eat at the picnic and he should be finishing up the report cards for the end of the year. The next morning he was off to the schoolhouse before I was out of bed, and when he returned he had little to say over supper, right after heading to the parlour and staying there until well after Alice and Louisa were tucked into bed. And so it went, day after day. I wouldn't mind if you stayed even five minutes for another cup of tea, I thought one evening, as he stood up from the table and was out of the kitchen and across the hall before I had a chance to refill his cup. It would be nice to talk to an adult for a few minutes longer, I sighed to myself as the parlour door closed. I know you have much to do before the end of the month but I could do with a bit of company.

Even after school finished I saw little of him, busy as he was working on a nearby farm to bring in some money over the summer. Not that it mattered much when he was home. *He may as well not be here,* I wrote one evening to Phoebe. *He rarely speaks except when one of us asks him a direct question, he eats what is put in front of him without commenting and vanishes after supper, either to the parlour or every few evenings 'to see some people' and leaves without saying where he's going. Planting time is past and harvest is not close at all. True, Robert was never one for idle talk but he is more unto himself than ever these days. He's so preoccupied. I wonder what's on his mind but I dare not ask. Likely he's missing Elizabeth even more, just wants to get away and forget things for a bit so best let him be. It was this time last year she passed on, do you remember? How things have changed since then for all of us! Oh well, dear Phoebe, better not to think about it for it makes me miss you and her and everyone else even more.*

With that I ended another letter home, taking up an envelope and writing out the address I knew from memory.

What to do now. I had finished reading the books I bought on the last excursion to Medicine Hat. The ironing was caught up, the kitchen neat and tidy. I never thought I would lack for things to do. Back in Inverness there was always somewhere to go, over to Phoebe's, the library, looking around the shops. And if I looked restless around home, Mother took care of that in short order; she always had a task or two at the ready. Maybe I could find a magazine in the parlour. As I stood up from the table and started towards the hall, something white hanging from a hook near the back door caught my eye. It was the sugar bag I was going to make into a tea cloth. Just before supper I had brought it in from the clothesline where I had hung it out that morning to bleach in the sun.

I decided I would rather start on the cloth than skim through magazines most of which I had read at least twice and, besides,

I didn't want to disturb Robert – he was home this evening, "going over some papers from the department," he said as he left the kitchen. Luck was with me; my sewing basket, usually kept in the parlour, was out in the kitchen, having been called into service for a bit of mending earlier in the day. Within a few minutes I was sitting down at the table once more, snipping open the seams of the bag and smoothing out the fabric. Let's see, what pattern should I use, I mused as I looked through the embroidery transfers I had ordered a few weeks ago from the *Medicine Hat News*. Here, this rose and butterfly design looks nice. Half an hour later several roses and butterflies were ironed around the edge of the square of cloth and it wasn't long before a pale pink rose emerged along the blue lines imprinted on one corner of the fabric, followed by a spray of lilacs and a bit of greenery. You'll regret this when the girls wake you up tomorrow morning, I said to myself, glancing up at the clock as I threaded my needle once again. But I like this too much to stop now.

Chapter Six

"Hello again. I haven't seen you for so long you may not remember me," a voice assailed me as I shepherded Emma and Fiona towards the till in the general store one afternoon in late July.

"Mrs. Taylor? Yes, it's been some time but of course I recall you. Where is Gregory?" I asked.

"'Off swimming in the creek with his cousins, which is a sensible thing to be doing on a day like today. How are you doing, and you and you?" she asked, leaning over and smiling at Alice and Louisa, who squirmed and retreated behind me.

"I'm doing well and so are the little ones – they're a wee bit shy," I got in before Mrs. Taylor resumed her barrage.

"I hope this heat isn't too much for you, although you'll wish it back once winter sets in. You missed the full brunt of it last year. I assume your brother is doing well; he should be with you to take care of the house and the girls. I hear he is seeing a lot of Miss Smythe the school teacher from over by Irvine way. Of course now that she is home for the summer she is much closer. Her parents' farm is just the other side of Diamond Coulee. Well, I must be getting along; Gregory and his cousins will be home for supper before I know it and my sister and I will have our hands full. Good to see you again and please give my best to your brother."

"Yes, yes, I will," I told her. She turned and left as suddenly as she had descended. "So that's what's been on Robert's mind," I said under my breath as I rounded the girls up and steered them towards the front counter.

"What's this I hear about you and Miss Smythe?" Robert looked up at me with a jolt.

"What, what do you mean?" he stammered as I glared at him.

"I took the girls to the store this afternoon. I just happened to run into Mrs. Taylor, a woman I met on the train. She tells me you have been seeing quite a bit of the teacher from Irvine."

"Yes, well, that is true I suppose," Robert mumbled, looking down at the newspaper he was reading when I strode into the room.

"You might have told me yourself, instead of leaving me to find out from that windbag," I hissed. "She caught me unawares; I felt such a fool. I wonder who else around here is gossiping behind my back."

"I, I was going to tell you, Grace, I just didn't know how to bring it up, that's all. It all started so suddenly and I haven't told anyone outright, nor have I written to Mother or Simon about Miss Smythe, for I wasn't sure they would approve," he said as he folded up the newspaper and laid it down on the kitchen table. Actually, Miss Smythe and her mother are coming here for tea this Sunday."

"And when were you planning to tell me about *that*, pray tell? As they were coming up the walk?" I countered. "I just might have had time to whip out the tea pot and slice some cake before they knocked on the door."

Robert shifted slightly in his chair and said in a voice so low I strained to hear him. "This whole matter has taken me by surprise almost as much as it has you." A pause, a long pause, followed. "I would appreciate your help on Sunday very much. Please, Grace." Another long pause.

"And you will have it, Robert," I replied.

Chapter Seven

Diamond Coulee, Alberta
January 10, 1923

Dear Phoebe,

We are in the midst of an enormous blizzard. It started shortly after Robert left for school this morning. The snow is so thick I can barely see the fence posts at the front and the shed at the back. Alice and Louisa are napping – I am surprised they could get off to sleep with the wind howling so. I have yet to see if Robert will make it home tonight. He had to stay at the school house one nasty night last month and I would not be surprised if he had to do the same tonight as this storm is stronger than anything I have seen here yet.

However, it is not the weather that concerns me most. There is something far more upsetting going on in my life. It concerns that woman I told you about before, Miss Smythe, the teacher Robert has been seeing for the last six months or so. They are going to be married! They told me on Boxing Day. The wedding is set for Easter. Miss Smythe – or Rosemary as she tells me to call her now – has lined up a replacement for her teaching position at Irvine School. This all has happened so quickly – it was just last June that I was introduced to her at the year-end picnic for the school district and now she is about to become my sister-in-law and she will be living under this roof.

No one has said anything more; so far the talk is all about the wedding arrangements, what the children will wear and what will be served at the reception… but I feel so uneasy. What becomes of me when Rosemary moves in and takes over? As Robert's wife she will have the upper hand and I don't care to be bossed around by her. Beyond that, I am wondering if this marriage is a good idea. I don't think I told you before that Rosemary was engaged to be married to a young farmer in the district who enlisted in the Great War and died early in the fighting, I think in 1915. I can understand she does not want to be left on the shelf and from her comments here and there I pick up that teaching was just something for her to do until she got married. Remember my cousin Gillian in Dingwall who lost her fiancé in the war? She found someone else a few years later; she told me when I was helping her get ready for her engagement party that it took her a while to get over losing Charles but eventually she realized she did not want to live on memories for the rest of her life. I was happy for her. I don't expect Robert to be alone forever yet I still feel that he needs more time to recover from losing Elizabeth.

I know this is Robert's business but his decisions directly affect me. He doesn't seem to be considering this and here I came all this way to help him when he really needed it. I am too confused to write more! Please bear with me and please write to me soon.

Your dear friend,
Grace

As it turned out Robert was storm-stayed at school after all. The blizzard kept on all evening, the howling winds scaring the little girls so much that I had to sit by their bedside until they fell asleep. When they finally nodded off I tucked the blankets around them snugly and tiptoed out of the bedroom, stepping quietly to the kitchen where I wandered about, straightening the tea towels and potholders by the stove and picking up a few pieces of bark that had fallen to the floor from the kindling box.

The evening yawned ahead. Most times I didn't mind being inside once darkness fell, but I had been indoors all day. Find something to do and do it, I told myself sternly; that's what Mum had to say when I complained about being bored.

"Where did I put my stitching?" I wondered aloud before crossing the hall to the parlour, where I found my sewing basket exactly where I had hidden it behind the armchair by the window so Alice would not see the doll I was making for her for her birthday. Returning to the kitchen, I settled beside the stove, threaded my needle with black floss and began outlining one of the eyes I had drawn on the doll's face a few days earlier. Hmm, shall I make her eyes brown or blue? I asked myself, poking through the mound of embroidery floss at the bottom of the basket. A skein of violet caught my eye. "Aha – perfect!" I exclaimed, yanking the floss free.

An hour later the wind was howling stronger than ever, the doll's eyes, nose and mouth were in place and I was examining my stock of thread for a length of bright pink. Rosy cheeks for this healthy young lady, I thought to herself, yawning as I looked at the clock. My goodness, it is nearly midnight. I wonder how I should dress this little one. I'll decide another day; I am so tired I can barely hold my needle. Good to be so tired. Straight to sleep tonight and no chance to worry about anything.

Chapter Eight

The doll went unclothed for some time. A few days after the blizzard cleared Robert and Rosemary announced their wedding plans – a ceremony at the Presbyterian manse in Diamond Coulee at two o'clock on the afternoon of February 27, followed by a small gathering at Rosemary's parents' home afterwards. I was so caught up sewing dresses for Alice and Louisa and an outfit for myself that I didn't have time to think about a wardrobe for a doll. It wasn't until nearly a week after the nuptials, which proceeded as arranged, the only exception being Alice and Louisa's tears bidding their father good-bye as he and Rosemary left for their honeymoon in Calgary and Robert's new mother-in-law curtly telling the girls to shush, that I had the time to resume work on the birthday present.

Good thing this does not have to be finished until June, I thought, as I took out my sewing basket after tucking the little ones in for their afternoon nap. At this rate it will take me until then to get it done. I wonder what Alice will call you, I asked myself as I pulled the doll from its hiding place under the parlour sofa and held it up to gauge the dimensions for the pinafore I was about to start. We'll just have to see, won't we?

Then I turned my attention to cutting out the blue plaid fabric discovered during a foray into Elizabeth's scrap box, the same place that had yielded a generous length of linen for the doll's body as well. Halfway through piecing the garment together an abrupt rap at the kitchen door startled me out of my concentration. Now who can that be? Visitors were few at the teacherage and usually known well in advance; the minister occasionally, the doctor when the girls were not well or maybe the district nurse, and that was about it. I unlatched the door and tried not to scowl when I saw who it was, for there stood Rosemary's mother bearing a large cardboard box.

"I have a few things," she said, pushing at the door with the carton, "two loaves of bread I made this morning, an orange chiffon cake and a jar of strawberry jam. Aren't you going to ask me in for a cup of tea? It's a rather cool wind that's blowing out there."

Barely into her first cup, Mrs. Smythe revealed another reason for her unscheduled visit. "Now that my daughter is going to be here there will not be much for you to do," she said briskly, helping herself to a piece of lemon loaf from the plate I had just set on the table.

"What… what do you mean?" I asked, although I was fairly certain what was in the air.

"Rosemary will be in charge, is what I mean. She can manage on her own," Mrs. Smythe said, swallowing the last bit of her tea and immediately reaching for the teapot.

"In other words, there's room in this house for one woman and not two," I suggested, firmly, returning my cup to my saucer firmly and reaching in front of Mrs. Smythe for the teapot.

"I don't think we need to be rude," Mrs. Smythe said, a faint flush creeping across her face.

"Well then, what do we need to do?" I asked.

"Sort things out, that's what," the older woman replied. "You'll be tripping over each other here. Now you know that I want what's best for all of you," she said, ignoring the cynical look on my face, continuing, "and I believe I have the solution. A friend of mine up near Bashaw is looking for a new domestic. The girl she had for three years just left to get married. It's a busy position – Dorothy, Mrs. MacDonald that is, is married to a doctor. They have a big house and yard to keep up. Their children are grown and gone but nonetheless, the MacDonalds have much to do, what with one thing and another, and they entertain frequently. Mrs. MacDonald needs help and it will be a good roof over your head and twenty dollars a month besides. There's many a girl who would welcome the chance to work there."

"Then let them!" I responded with a snort. "I came here to look after my brother's children after their mother died, not to be a servant girl."

"And now your brother has another wife to take care of him and his family," Mrs. Smythe said, sliding another slice of lemon loaf onto her plate.

"Then send me home," I responded in a flash.

"We haven't the money, Grace. Neither Robert nor Rosemary, nor you nor I for that matter, can pay your passage back to Scotland now. We will save what we can and you can put aside some of your own earnings and you will be able to go home in a year or two. Time passes quickly."

"That's decent of you, I must say. It's my life and everyone else is deciding it for me!" I said, a swift fury overtaking my earlier unease. "You have the nerve!"

"I am just being realistic, Grace," Mrs. Smythe said, pushing herself away from the table, sending the teacups rattling. "I believe my husband is out front to get me and I hear the wee ones stirring."

"No wonder. The racket you made shoving your chair across the floor was enough to wake the dead," I said as I stood and started clearing the table.

"That will be enough, Grace. I'll see myself out," the older woman said, reaching over to collect her hat and coat from the counter where she had dropped them after inviting herself in. "Please try to understand; this is the best we can do given the circumstances."

As the dreadful day wound down I found myself more and more distracted, barely able to assemble supper, trying to keep my wrath from the girls, so caught up in my despair I couldn't pay much attention to their chatter.

"Auntie, do you think they will bring us anything?" Alice asked midway through the meal.

"We shall have to wait and see, won't we," I replied, adding, "I wouldn't count on it," under my breath. That evening I did something I thought I would never do. Once the little ones were in bed I went into the parlour and rummaged through Robert's desk, looking for evidence as to who had hatched the plot to get rid of me. Was it Rosemary's idea or was Robert in on it, is what I wanted to know. I found my answer soon enough in a letter shoved under a sheaf of correspondence from the school district. The letter was from our mother.

I gasped when I read it. Not only did Mother know of the impending plan to re-locate me without my consent – a plan devised by both Robert and Rosemary as it turned out – Mother approved of it, pleading lack of funds due to bills still out-standing from Father's long stay in hospital. "There is no other recourse but for Grace to remain in Canada and work at the job you have arranged. I haven't the money to pay for her return passage," she had written. So that was why my dear brother told me not to worry about collecting the mail, that he would get away from work early a few times a week. Expecting some important papers from the department in Edmonton, he said.

Liar! I sat down and put my head on the desk and cried. First my brother conspires with his soon-to-be wife to turn me out, then Mother goes back on her word... who in this world can I trust?

I was still fuming when the newlyweds returned the next day. Somehow I managed to hold my tongue until supper was over and the girls tucked up in bed. I was out in the back porch getting more wood for the stove when I heard Robert come into the kitchen.

"It took a while but I think the little ones are settled," he said to Rosemary who was sitting at the table scanning the newspapers from the previous week.

"That's good, dear," Rosemary replied. "I think I'll go to the parlour and write a few letters. I need to thank my aunt for the tablecloth she sent us and your superintendent's wife for the cream and sugar set."

Good, she's out of the way, I thought. All the better to have it out with Robert. I took a deep breath, kicked the partly closed door open wide, marched into the kitchen, dropped the wood into the box beside the stove, then turned around to face my brother.

The discussion began calmly enough. Keeping my voice down so Rosemary wouldn't hear, I asked, "Exactly what is going on Robert?"

"What do you mean?" he responded.

"I think you know what I mean," I countered. "I hear that I am being turned out."

I must confess I lost my temper, I wrote Phoebe the next day. *He insisted he didn't know Mrs. Smythe would be coming over, that he intended to talk to me himself. I told him I didn't believe that for a minute, that I think he's a cad for sending me away like this and he is breaking the agreement under which I came to Canada. I reminded him I was to be a housekeeper and nanny for him, not a servant for someone I don't even know. Rosemary heard the row and came running into the kitchen, telling me to stop it right away. I lit into her and let her know what I thought of her and her mother. Rosemary informed me I was to pack my bags right away; in the morning she would call her father to take me to the train station and I would be on my way to my new residence, as she called it, and she would have her mother tell my new employer that I was en route. Nasty, the whole encounter was, and Robert just sat there. I am so disappointed in him, so disgusted.*

Chapter Nine

Misty River, Alberta,
June 8, 1923

Dearest Phoebe,

How lovely to hear from you so soon. My spirits perked up the instant I saw the envelope with your handwriting on it. Given my abrupt departure from Diamond Coulee I am surprised I thought to include my new address when I scribbled that letter to you while I was at the station in Calgary waiting for the train for Bashaw. I was in such a state. At first it was just a relief to be away from Robert and Rosemary but then the strain of not knowing what lay ahead set in. Not that I didn't feel that way when I left Inverness but at least I knew the person I was going to, or at least I thought I did – after all this I'm not sure of anything anymore. The stopover in Calgary was the longest two hours of my life, sitting there wondering what was to become of me. My apprehension must have shown because the person who met me at Bashaw and took me to Misty River, James, the handyman for the MacDonalds, told me to 'cheer up and not mind the missus – her bark is worse than her bite.'

I'm not so sure about that but… At any rate, I must tell you about my new surroundings. I have a room to myself, not a very big room – even so, it's nice to have territory of my own after sharing sleeping quarters with two little ones, much as I miss Alice and Louisa, and my new room is right off the kitchen, so it is warm enough and when it is hot in the summer I can sleep on the couch in the back porch. Best of all, it puts some distance between myself and the owners – I am still adjusting to living with strangers for the first time in my life.

The house is large – a palace compared to the teacherage. The kitchen alone is bigger than the previous kitchen and parlour put together. There is a separate dining room (also a good size), a parlour for the missus, and a den, where the man of the house and his friends 'retire' as they put it (take refuge from their wives is more like it). Upstairs there are three bedrooms and a bathroom. Quite a fancy place it is, nicely done throughout, with fine furniture in all the rooms and paintings on the walls and two full bookshelves in the den.

I only wish I could take to my new employers as much as I have taken to their house. The doctor is a gruff sort who grunts his words more often than not. To be fair, I do not see all that much of him; briefly at breakfast and then he is off to his office on the main street. He reappears at suppertime. He is out most evenings, if not tending to a patient then he is at some kind of meeting – Masons or Elks – and he frequently gets together with his gentlemen friends to play Chinese checkers and whist.

Mrs. M. is a brisk woman who has no trouble expressing herself. She talks for both of them, enunciating her words in a shrill voice I detest already. She loves nothing more than to order me about; indeed, I think she lies in bed at night composing my list of duties for the next day. When I think of how I used to run my brother's home...true, the days were long oftentimes, and it got tiresome having only young children to talk with most of the time, but Alice and Louisa appreciated what I did for them, they were affectionate and they are family. I would gladly go without my salary and my own room to see them smile and hear their sweet voices and most of all, to be able to decide what needs to be done and when to do it.

Oh I am prattling on just like the missus. I must let you go before I bore you to tears with my complaining. I promise to be more cheerful next time. I hope to hear from you soon. A letter from you brings such sunshine into my life.

Much love,
Grace

Right away I addressed an envelope, stuffed the letter into it and sealed the envelope firmly. Wouldn't want this to be seen before it reaches its proper destination, I thought, setting the envelope out on my dresser to remind me to take it to the post office the next day on my afternoon off. I looked at the clock on the dresser. Nearly four o'clock... time to bring in the wash and get going on supper. The missus had choir practice that evening and Dr. M. some kind of meeting to attend. Supper must not be late.

Though it very nearly was... As I took the clothes down from the line, something at the closest corner of the yard caught my eye, a plant of some sort, a cluster of pink and green stalks, topped by frowsy leaves from last year it looked like. I had noticed the plant that morning when I was pegging out the wash but had to hurry inside at Mrs. M.'s beckoning and could not investigate further. I'll take a minute now, I figured, tucking the last of the laundry into the basket and placing the bag of clothespins on top. I crossed the yard and bent down to the curious clump of I-wasn't-sure-what, pulling aside the wilted stalks and dead leaves so brittle they disintegrated at my touch. "Rhubarb!" I exclaimed, a smile spreading across my face. I set the laundry basket down and began clearing the lifeless growth. Before I could finish Mrs. M. found me and started ranting, reaming me out for the slow start to the meal.

"And on this day of all days, with such a busy evening ahead – why are you wool-gathering out here when there's so much to be done inside..."

I knew by now that once the missus got going she was unstoppable, like a locomotive gathering steam to reach full throttle. The best course of action was to apply myself to the tasks at hand, which I did, murmuring, "Yes, ma'am" and "Of course" to Mrs. M.'s barked commands, and soon enough the meal was on the table – five minutes late, mind you. Not long after the master and lady of the house hurried off to their activities, though not soon enough for me, even if I did have the dining room table to clear and the kitchen to clean up.

Early the next morning I slipped out to the back yard to tend to my discovery, pulling out the dead stalks to let the sun reach the unfurled yellow-green leaves and pink stems underneath the remnants of last season. Some rain that evening and a few nights afterwards, a bit more weeding and a new crop of rhubarb was well underway. One afternoon a few weeks later when Mrs. M. was out at yet another meeting – the temperance women or whatever – I harvested an armful of bright red stalks, hurrying back into the house to stir the chicken stew bubbling on top of the kitchen stove.

"Mind the stew doesn't burn," Mrs. M. had called out as she headed off. "Add a bit more broth in an hour or so. And add it slowly so it doesn't splash over onto the floor; we just cleaned yesterday."

I cleaned yesterday was more like it. *You* sat and drank I don't know how many cups of tea because your arm was aching – the rain brought your rheumatism on, so you said.

"And remember, Dr. MacDonald has his Masons' meeting this evening, so we will have to have dinner on the table in good time."

I will have to have dinner on the table in good time, I thought, but said, "Yes, Mrs. MacDonald," adding under my breath, "and I will have a surprise for you," as I took the pastry board down from the top cupboard and searched through the drawer underneath for the rolling pin. Dusting both lightly with flour, I rolled out the pastry dough I had made earlier and stowed in the icebox in a dampened tea cloth. Next I lined a small pie pan with the dough and turned my attention to the bundle of rhubarb stashed in the bread bin at the bottom of the bank of drawers under the kitchen counter. Within minutes a plump rhubarb tart was baking in the oven.

The impromptu dessert went over well – after a while, that is. "And what might this be?" Mrs. MacDonald inquired as I set two plates, each bearing a good-sized slice of the pastry, on the table.

"It is rhubarb tart, with rhubarb from your own garden, Mrs. MacDonald. The crumb cake we were to have seemed a bit stale."

"So you took it upon yourself to make something else without asking," Mrs. Macdonald replied. "And suppose the doctor and I do not care for rhubarb?" she asked, her cheeks flushing as she dealt out each word more sharply than the one before.

"Oh leave it be, Dorothy," said her husband, who had already pulled one of the dessert plates over and was well into his portion. "You know very well we both like rhubarb and this is delicious. Please bring me more, Grace."

Which I did, hurrying to the kitchen in a daze.

I'd never heard him say so much at one time to anyone, and didn't he stop the missus in her tracks, I relayed to Phoebe in my next letter.

Later that evening, while washing the tart pan, I remembered with a start when I last made the same dessert. The school picnic at Diamond Coulee; was it really just last year? It seems so long ago, I mused, smiling just a little as I recalled that afternoon by the river. Mrs. M. might not have been lavish with her compliment about my unscheduled dish, 'acceptable,' she called it. Can praise be so faint I wonder? Still it was better than what that shrew of a principal's wife had to say.

And then before I could head it off, a rush of memories rolled over me, as sure and unbeatable as the tide on the River Ness that Phoebe and I had watched come in so many times. Go away, go away, I ordered my jumbled thoughts, but they were determined to stick in my mind – the walks with Phoebe over the wide bridge that crossed the river to our part of Inverness, Mother and Phoebe waving me off at the train station, the rough crossing on the boat and the endless train journey across the prairies… "I do not want to think of this; I cannot," I whispered, reaching out for a tea towel to wipe my eyes. "I must finish this up before *they* come home," I told myself as I resumed the washing up, pushing my homesick thoughts to the back of my mind, knowing full well they would be back when I least wanted them.

It felt so good being out in the yard that whenever Mrs. M. was away for a few hours I slipped out back to catch some fresh air and poke around what I figured was once a garden patch. "Too late to plant anything other than lettuce this year and, please God, I do not want to be here next year for spring seeding; but in the meantime, these flowers could do with a bit of attention," I murmured to myself, pulling a weed here and there from the flower bed that ran alongside the white picket fence at the side of the property. Another month or maybe less and these delphiniums will be out in bloom, I thought as I worked my way along the fence, digging out dandelions and clumps of crab grass from between the posts.

"I see someone has been busy in the yard," Dr. MacDonald commented as I cleared the soup bowls from the table that evening.

"Grace, was it you?" Mrs. M. asked as I re-entered the dining room with the roast and vegetables.

"Yes, ma'am, I had a bit of time and thought I would tend to the flowers."

"I had to let it slide this year," Mrs. M. said in an awkward tone. "I cannot do much of that sort of thing, what with the arthritis in my knees and wrists."

Perhaps if you rid yourself of some of that extra weight you are carrying you would be more agile, I thought, as I headed to the kitchen to see to tea and dessert. And then what would your excuse be?

After that I escaped to the yard whenever I could. I liked neatening up the flower beds the way I used to in Grandmother Sinclair's minute yard in Inverness, and with a bit of coaxing the roses and hollyhocks blossomed despite the overwhelming dry heat that enveloped the area that summer. For once Mrs. M. had little to say about what I was doing; indeed, as the summer wore on and the plants came into full flower Mrs. M. took up the kitchen chores some afternoons and let me stay out weeding, clipping and pruning, which suited me. Nice to be away from her clutches, I thought, one such afternoon, humming as I pinched the stem of a thistle plant between my thumb and index finger and tugged at the root, tossing the stubborn weed into the wheelbarrow beside me. Let's see, what else needs to be done. Oh yes, the delphiniums and the Maltese cross need to be staked, they've grown so tall they'll be bending over before we know it.

Chapter Ten

"I must say, Dorothy, your flowers are looking very nice."

Which one of the Women's Institute members said it I couldn't be sure – I barely caught the comment as I was leaving the parlour en route to the kitchen to make more tea. I hoped it was Mrs. Wilson, much admired for her green thumb. There was a good turnout at the Women's Institute meeting that day, despite the sticky heat and the menacing storm clouds looming overhead. The ladies were keen to hear about the new doctor soon to take up practice with Dr. MacDonald. So was I, as the missus and her husband had not discussed the matter in my hearing. I hurried back into the parlour as quickly as I could while balancing a tray laden with a full teapot and two milk pitchers and sugar bowls.

"He's from Stettler," Mrs. M. said, her voice perking up as the others stopped talking and focused on her. "His name is Ian Robertson. His father is Dr. Neil Robertson, who trained with my husband." Mrs. M. paused to sip her tea.

"And does he have a family?" someone asked.

"He recently was married to a young lady he met overseas while he was in the medical corps during the war," Mrs. M. continued. "He met her at the home of one of his great-aunts he was visiting in Edinburgh while he was on leave."

This was getting interesting. I approached Mrs. M. and offered to warm her tea. "They wrote back and forth after he came home and resumed his studies in Edmonton." Mrs. M. stopped for another sip of tea.

"Do go on, Dorothy," someone urged, as if Mrs. M. needed encouragement.

"Well, after his graduation he decided to go over to Scotland to see her and while he was there he proposed marriage."

"My goodness," murmured one woman.

"You don't say," chirped another.

"They were wed a few weeks later, a small ceremony at the bride's home. Dr. Neil and his wife say they don't mind not being there, they understand and all, but you do wonder," Mrs. M. said, arching her eyebrows and pursing her lips before shifting her look my way and motioning towards the nearly bare cake plate on the table beside the sofa.

"And what might the bride's name be?" asked one of the women as I picked up the plate.

"Her first name is Catherine; her maiden name has slipped my mind, but that's no matter, now she is Mrs. Robertson, of course," Mrs. M. replied, returning her teacup to its saucer and fixing her gaze on the plate in my hand.

"Oh yes," I mumbled, scurrying to the kitchen where I sliced more cherry pound cake, layered the plate and hastened back to the parlour just in time to hear one of the guests, Mrs. Foster, say, "I would like to have a tea to welcome her," to which Mrs. M. replied stiffly, "I believe that will be up to me."

As it turned out, Mrs. Foster had her way. A domestic crisis at Mrs. MacDonald's daughter's in Red Deer – *or something Madame perceived as a crisis* – I later wrote to Phoebe – took the woman of the house away, initially for a week that stretched into ten blessed days – *for once I could hear myself think, with no one bossing me about; how I wish it could go on forever. It is so difficult to live with someone who keeps at you every minute of the day* – but all too soon the missus was back and furious on hearing at the Women's Institute meeting two days after her return that a fellow W.I. member had beaten her to it in welcoming the new doctor's wife.

"It should have been at *my* home," Mrs. M. fumed as she stormed into the foyer and through to the kitchen after the meeting. "Grace, let's hurry and get supper started. Have you brought in the wash? Did James come by to fix the latch on the shed door as I asked?"

"Yes to both, Mrs. MacDonald," I replied, retreating to the chair by the corner of the stove to shell the peas. "And James saw to the rotted out step on the back stoop while he was at it."

"Well, that's *something* good that's come of today," Mrs. M. groused. "I've been after him to attend to the shed door for ever so long, and here he's done the back step to boot." For a moment the thunderous look eased from Mrs. M.'s face, but two seconds later there it was again. "One thing for sure, I'll not let Anne Foster get the better of me," she said as she picked up the bowl of icing I had just finished making. "I'll hold an at home that no one will forget for a good long time," she muttered, taking up a dinner knife and slathering the frosting in broad waves across the spice cake I had baked earlier in the day.

A few weeks later a notice in the village weekly beckoned 'all ladies of the community to come out and greet the new doctor's bride at the home of Mrs. Duncan MacDonald from 1 p.m. to 3 p.m. on Tuesday the twelfth of September.'

Such scrubbing, dusting and polishing – you would think the Queen of England was coming to visit, and the endless baking – lemon squares, butter tarts and four kinds of cake at least, I passed on to Phoebe. *But finally I will see this person from our homeland.*

And speak with her as well, which happened after Mrs. MacDonald dispatched me to refill the new Mrs. Robertson's teacup. "Would you care for milk and sugar, ma'am?" I asked, trying not to smile at the newcomer's startled look on hearing a familiar accent. "Oh dear, the milk is almost gone. I will be right back with more," I said, bustling off to the kitchen.

As I took the pitcher of milk from the icebox I heard footsteps behind me. It was Mrs. Robertson, who smiled warmly and asked, "And where might you be from?"

"Inverness, ma'am."

"And so am I!" she declared, her eyes lighting up. "What part of the city?"

But before I could answer Mrs. M. was in the kitchen, eyes darting, a weak smile barely masking the black look threatening to overtake her face. "We will be out in a second with more tea, Mrs. Robertson," the missus managed, nodding towards the parlour. "And what do you think you are doing, young lady, speaking with the company?" she hissed, the moment Mrs. Robertson departed the kitchen. "That's not your place."

"Cook, clean, follow orders – that's my place," I muttered to myself as I tackled the stack of cups and saucers waiting for me after the last of the guests left. A few words with someone from the same place… you'd think I was starting a revolution the way the old bat carried on.

"What's that you said?" a familiar voice asked.

"You startled me," I breathed out after turning around to find James standing inside the kitchen door. "I was just going on to myself about the rebuke I received this afternoon from Mrs. M. Apparently it does not do to speak to the new doctor's wife, even if she starts the conversation."

James shook his head and smiled. "Ah yes, the missus is only too willing to remind people like us who is boss and what is right and what is wrong, according to her that is. That's the way she is and always will be. I was just dropping off the lumber for the window sills I'm making for the back porch. You wouldn't have a bit of tea left, would you?" he asked, pulling a chair over by the stove. "Ah, that feels good," he sighed as he settled onto the chair, holding his hands out towards the heat. "Been a long day."

After a few minutes he pulled his arms back, dropped his hands down and started cracking his knuckles.

"James, if you do not stop that immediately I shall go berserk and choke you," I said, sending a menacing look his way.

"Then get me that cup of tea," he countered.

"Anything to stop that," I said, handing him the mug I had just filled.

"You know, it wouldn't hurt for you to get out a bit more, old girl," he said as he polished off the butter tarts I rustled up for him along with the requested cuppa. "What would you say if my nephew William, you remember I introduced him to you last week when he came out here to help me put up the new fence; well, what if he were to ask you to accompany him to the movie at the Majestic Theatre in Bashaw next week? I believe he had his eye on you, young lady," he said.

"I.. I don't think so," I stammered, staring into my own mug of tea.

"Not even if it's *The Last of the Mohicans* that's playing?" James asked. "Why it's a wonderful film, very dramatic, I saw it when it first came to the Majestic two years ago. It was so popular the theatre got it back. I've a good mind to see it again myself."

"No, I don't think so," I repeated. "I really must get on with the washing up."

It's not that I wouldn't like seeing this movie I've heard so much about, and I've heard plenty about the theatre in Bashaw as well; it sounds like quite the place for a small town, I wrote to Phoebe a few days later. It's just that I see no point in encouraging anyone when I am not staying here for good.

And I do hope it will not be too long before we are together. I miss our walks along the river and through town, going to the library and the news agent's and looking in the shop windows. Here there are so few places to go and no one to chum with. The only person who is friendly to me is the young doctor's wife. She smiles at me after church, and stops to chat when she runs into me in the grocery store or at the post office. She seems rather lonely. It is too bad we cannot get together – I think we would both enjoy it – but ye gods, I would never hear the end of it from Mrs. M.

My goodness, I did not intend to go on so long! The missus is out at one of her meetings and for once didn't leave me a list of jobs to do in her absence. Tonight it's a WCTU meeting; you know, those women who campaign against alcohol. Mrs. M. goes on and on at me about the evils of drink but maybe she should take a closer look at what's happening in her own home. I swear I smelled liquor when I went in to tidy up the den after Dr. M. had his friend Dr. Anderson the dentist over tonight. The odor from the glasses they'd been drinking from reminded me of the brandy Mother puts in the sauce for the Christmas pudding. Oh well, that is not my concern.

It's so nice to visit with you, one-sided though it is. I must let you go. My best to you and all your family.

Your loving friend,
Grace

Chapter Eleven

18 Castle Street,
Edinburgh, Scotland,
August 2, 1924

My Dear Grace,

I do not like to be the bearer of bad tidings but there is something you must know. Our beloved mother departed this life two weeks ago, on the 18th day of July, peacefully t home. Her service was held at our church on July 22nd and she is now buried beside Father in Knox Presbyterian Cemetery.

Mother had not been well for some time. At first we thought it was melancholy stemming from Father's death but it became apparent in the last few months it was more than that. Dr. Bowen had been summoned several times and was of the opinion it was her heart that was ailing her. He recommended bed rest and was in the midst of determining a course of medication when Mother took a turn for the worse and slipped away before anything more could be done.

I am settling the estate forthwith, as there are still bills outstanding from Father's untimely passing. The house on Seawall Lane soon will be put up for sale. I dread seeing our family home pass from us but there is no other way to deal with our parents' debts.

I hope that you are in good health, dear sister, and faring well in your new position. I was surprised to learn of your departure from Robert's home and your move to Misty River. His card at Christmas did not say much and neither did yours. I have written to Robert and Rosemary informing them of the sad news.

I think of you often, Grace, and wish you could have attended my wedding last fall. I think you would get on well with my wife. Her family have been very good to me all along and especially during these last difficult days. I hope to see you again sometime soon so that you can meet my lovely Jane. In the meantime, we send you our best and I remain,

Your brother,
Simon

"Oh no, this cannot be so… I do not believe it," I whispered as tears started down my face, two drops landing near the bottom of the page, almost obliterating Simon's signature from the nubby beige paper. After reading my brother's letter a third time, I wiped my face with my apron, folded the page in half and then half again, lifted myself off the edge of my bed and placed the letter underneath the pillow. On the other side of the bedroom door I heard rustlings in the kitchen – the tap running, a pot being filled and placed on the stove, a drawer pulled open and a turbulent search underway for one utensil or another. A glance at the clock on the bedside table, half past four, I have to help Mrs. M. get supper. I wiped my eyes again and stepped out into the kitchen.

At first Mrs. MacDonald was too busy at the sink and cutting board to notice anything was amiss. It was only after I came in from the pantry with a jar of fruit preserves that Mrs. M. looked up. "And what's the matter with you?" she demanded.

"It's… it's my mother. She passed on back in July. I just received word today from my brother in Scotland," I said, my voice dwindling to almost nothing. To my surprise, Mrs. M. took the jar from my hands and told me I'd best go and lie down.

"The doctor and I will manage fine tonight. I am sorry about your mother."

I stumbled to my room and sat on the end of the bed, staring into space for I don't know how long.

Dreams invaded my sleep that night and several thereafter. The first, the most vivid, brought back that faraway day when I waved Elizabeth and Robert and their little one off at the train station in Inverness, Mother by my side. As the train faded into the distance I woke to see the full moon casting its light between the undrawn curtains. Gathering up the patchwork quilt folded at the end of the bed, I pulled the chair from the far corner of the room and sat at the window, wrapping the quilt around my shoulders as I gazed at the moon, wondering if it was casting the same light across my parents' graves. "I hope so," I murmured to myself. After a while, a long while, I unwrapped myself and went back to bed. Another dream imprinted itself on my sleep – this time I was on the train, and it was Mother on the platform, waving furiously and trying her best to smile amidst the tears streaming down her face.

Chapter Twelve

Misty River, Alberta,
September 23, 1924

Dear Phoebe,

    Thank you for your detailed letter telling me of Mother's funeral, and for remembering me to the friends who gathered after the service. I wish so much I could have been there but it helps knowing that you were there for me. You are a true friend.

    Now more than ever I wish we could be together. There is no one here for me to talk to, really talk to. When I first received Simon's letter I was shocked, now I am overwhelmingly sad that I will never see Mother again. Besides that, I feel so lost. When I lost one parent I felt unbalanced; now that both are gone a sense of formlessness, of not belonging somehow, has taken over. I move through each day doing what is expected of me; for once I am glad of the routine. I try hard not to dwell on the past and I will not let myself think of the future – I stamp that out as soon as it comes to mind.

    Nighttime is altogether different. I am so restless; it takes forever to get to sleep and when I finally do, often I am plagued by dreams, almost always disturbing. Such a troubling start to the day, to awake and have to clear your mind from what prevailed upon you during the night. But then last night a dream of a different kind happened – I dreamed I heard my mother's voice – I could not see her but I heard her as clear as could be. She told me she is happy in Heaven and not to worry about her. I woke up feeling odd but in a way comforted and the feeling stays with me still. If the dreams are to continue, may they be as reassuring as this latest one.

Yesterday was my afternoon off. I was feeling listless, wondering what to do. James was not around so I could not hop a lift into Bashaw. I poked around the public library for a wee while and when I came out it was such a nice day I decided to walk around for a bit. I started along the street behind the library and kept going until the road ended on the outskirts of town where I saw a sign pointing to the cemetery. I had never been there but as it was close by I decided to go and have a look. It turned out to be larger than I thought and rather pretty, with trees and shrubs throughout and a nice wrought iron fence encircling it. The gate was unlocked so I went in and roamed around. In one corner I spied a headstone for a woman who was born the same year as Mother. However, the woman buried here has been gone for twelve years. Perhaps her husband has re-married or has moved away, as the grave looks to have been left untended for a long time. I returned to the MacDonalds' and got a bag and a few gardening tools out of the shed and went back to the cemetery, where I weeded that unkempt plot and trimmed the grass around the stone. It looked so much nicer. I will try to keep it up during the good weather, maybe even sneak a few flowers from the back garden and place them in a jar of water in front of the headstone. If I can't do that for Mother, I can do it for someone else.

Last week the minister stopped in and had tea with me in the kitchen. I didn't think he really knew me, his smile and handshake after church each week seemed rather vague but he actually does know quite a bit about me – he is aware of my background and why I came to Canada in the first place. At any rate, it was a pleasant visit.

A few days ago I received a letter from Robert of all people; the first from him since he and Rosemary turned me out. He tells me he has been promoted to principal of the new school over by Irvine effective the new school year and he and Rosemary and the girls will be moving over the summer. They are expecting a child in January. I suppose I will look in the general store in Bashaw for something to send the new baby; that's if Robert and Rosemary bother to inform me of the little one's birth. It wouldn't surprise me if they didn't, nothing would surprise me about Robert, influenced as he is by his vile new wife and her even viler mother.

The staccato buzz of the front doorbell interrupted my letter-writing. Who can that be? I wondered as I shuffled to the foyer. The groceries were delivered this morning and there's no company due that I've been informed of. I opened the door to find the new doctor's wife standing on the veranda. "Oh, how are you, Mrs. Robertson? Good to see you," I said, greatly surprised. "Mrs. MacDonald is not at home."

"That is all right," Mrs. Robertson said softly. "It is you I have come to see. We have been away and I've only just heard the sad news about your mother. I wanted to tell you how sorry I am," she said, taking something small and gift-wrapped from her bag and handing it over to me. 'Take care of yourself, my dear,' she said, touching my shoulder lightly before she turned and headed down the steps.

I went back inside the house and stood in the foyer for I do not know how long, looking down at the pretty tissue paper and ribbon-bedecked package, thinking about Mrs. Robertson's kind gesture, I continued my letter to Phoebe. *Now I must end this and get out to the kitchen to get a few things done. Thank you again for your help during this unhappy time.*

Love to you and yours,
Grace

I had no sooner finished the letter than the missus returned from whatever social engagement had taken her away and soon after began the rush of preparations for the evening meal.

In this case the pace cranked up a few notches due to another commitment Mrs. MacDonald had to be off to in a few hours. Thank goodness I had time to get the present – which turned out to be a bar of lavender-scented Yardley soap – tucked away in the top drawer of my dresser, I thought, as I moved about the kitchen, gathering up lettuce and tomatoes from the colander in the sink and depositing them on the cutting board, chopping the greens ferociously before tossing them into the salad bowl. I do not need a lecture on the inappropriateness of contact between myself and the new doctor's wife, 'even if you are from the same area.'

Chapter Thirteen

The days went on, and on, one day hardly differing from another, at least that's how it seemed. Get up in the morning, get dressed, braid my hair and coil it into place – Mrs. M. could not, would not, tolerate 'a messy mop' on top of my head – make my bed and hustle into the kitchen for another day of making meals, sweeping, dusting, beating out the carpets, except for Mondays, when laundry dominated the day. What a pain that was. No more absconding to the yard; the chilly fall weather put an end to that once I raked the leaves and cut down the perennials. Of course, there was my afternoon off a week, although there's so little to do after stopping by the cemetery to make sure all was in order at the grave I had adopted. I usually I ended up spending the rest of the afternoon in my room, reading or stitching. Once in a while I made it into Bashaw to look around their main street, and I did see *The Last of the Mohicans* after all, sitting by myself at the back of the theatre. A good movie, I could see why it was brought back for another run.

Be careful what you wish for, Grandma Sinclair told me so many times, a thought that came back to me when my boredom broke in a way I never imagined. A month and a half after the sad news from home the MacDonalds' house caught fire.

The place did not burn down but there was extensive damage, I relayed
to Phoebe. *Earlier in the evening Mrs. MacDonald went off to one of her
meetings and it was the doctor's turn to host his Mason committee meeting.
His friend, that lecherous Mr. Stephenson – you never want to be alone
with him I found out lately, after he followed me into the pantry and got
uncomfortably close – stayed after the others left and the two were having
a right good time, talking and laughing, getting louder and louder, until the
missus arrived home. That put a damper on the goings on. For once I was
glad to see her – I was so tired I just wanted to collect the dishes, tidy up
and get off to bed. Definitely not tea those two chums were imbibing, as
was usually the case when they got together. I think Mrs. M. caught on
because she gathered up the tumblers and plates from the doctor's desk
herself and waved me off to my room.*

*Not long after everyone turned in I was startled out of my sleep by
crackling sounds. I smelled smoke right away and thought it was the kitchen
stove. When I opened my bedroom door there was such a wall of smoke I
could barely see. I fumbled my way into the kitchen, groped around for a
tea towel and sprinkled it with water from the tank at the end of the stove,
put the towel over my nose and mouth and hurried past the dining room
to the staircase. As I ran up the stairs I looked back to see flames eating
away at the bottom at the door to the den. I roused the MacDonalds and
by the time I got them awake and mobile the fire had spread through much
of the main floor. We heard shouts from the back yard and followed the
noise to the other side of the upper hallway. The doctor pulled the window
open and would you know, there was a ladder someone had put to the ledge
underneath the window and that is how we got out. There we were, standing about on the front lawn, wrapped in blankets some good soul provided
us, everyone watching the flames pursue their relentless course. The fire
brigade arrived soon after and managed to stop the house from being totally
destroyed and the fire from spreading to other properties.*

*Not to worry, I was not long without a roof over my head. A young
constable with the Royal Canadian Mounted Police asked me if I was all
right and if there was anyone he could contact for me. I asked him if he*

would take me please to the Robertsons' house – you know, the new doctor and his lovely wife I told you about. The words were scarcely out of my mouth when who did we see but Dr. Robertson amidst the crowd. He spotted me at the same time and straight away he was over, offering to take me to his house even before I asked. When we arrived Mrs. Robertson had the guest room ready for me.

I slept well into the morning and awoke to find breakfast waiting for me in the dining room. After pouring me a second cup of tea Mrs. Robertson approached the matter of what I might do next. Apparently the word was out already that the damage is so severe that the MacDonalds are having the house pulled down and a new one built on the same site. (Dr. Robertson had called while I was still sleeping and filled his wife in on the details.) Apparently during the rebuilding Mrs. M. is going to stay with her daughter at Red Deer while Dr. M. remains here to keep up his practice, staying with one of his Mason friends. There was also talk that the MacDonalds were not quite sure what I was to do until the new house is ready but thought something could be worked out as to a temporary position in Red Deer and then I would re-join them when their new place is ready. I was having none of that! I told Mrs. Robertson I wanted to move on and asked her to help me find a new position. She smiled and said she would be happy to do so.

What a nice woman – I will miss her, and James as well. I do not know where your next letter from me will come from, dear Phoebe, only that you will hear from me no matter what. Write to me here; Mrs. Robertson will forward your letter on. I hope to be settled somewhere soon and I promise to let you know where I am so that we do not lose contact.

In the meantime, I send my best,

With much love,
Grace

Chapter Fourteen

Here we go again. Third time I've done this, riding the train across the prairie to a place I've never been, only to a much bigger place for a change. Like last time I'm going to an employer I do not know and I can't help feeling a bit apprehensive, much as I trust Mrs. Robertson to refer me to a place where I will get on well. I hope so, I hope I'm not going from the frying pan into the fire, I thought as the train pulled into the South Edmonton station.

Edmonton, Alberta,
November 17, 1924

Dear Phoebe,

I have so much to tell you. Mrs. Robertson sent on your letter as she said she would. Better yet she found me a new position through a friend of her mother's. The friend moved to Canada several years ago but Mrs. Robertson remembers her well from Inverness and has been to see her in Edmonton. The family friend knew one of her neighbours was needing a domestic. The friend said her neighbor is a kind person and a fair employer; the girl she had had been with her for four years but was leaving to get married – that keeps happening doesn't it? – so I chanced it and accepted the job and I'm glad I did, for I am in a much, much happier situation than before. Indeed, I have to pinch myself to believe that this is really me, that my life has taken such a good turn.

My new employers, Mr. and Mrs. Logan, are Canadians of Scottish descent. Mr. Logan – his first name is Evan – is tall, bearded and quite outgoing. His parents emigrated from the Highlands a few years before the Great War. He followed in his father's footsteps, becoming a lawyer, and is well-known in Edmonton, which is the capital city of Alberta. He has a busy practice; he sets off to work early each morning, umbrella and briefcase under his arm, out to catch the streetcar to take him downtown to his office. He puts in a full day and frequently goes out in the evenings to various meetings but he always takes time to speak to me when I bring in the evening meal. He loves to read and brings books home every other day it seems. The shelves in his den are jammed and there are books piled everywhere in the master bedroom.

Mrs. Logan's first name is Isla, and her people are from Glasgow. She is a short, ample person with a ready smile, a rather quiet sort but friendly and well-meaning. She has high standards for everything – the house and yard must always be in order, and she does not tolerate any shortcuts when it comes to the tasks she assigns me. When she tells me to 'take the cloth and Swedish oil to the banisters on the front staircase,' she checks afterward to make sure I have not missed a single edge or corner. Nonetheless she is never unpleasant when correcting me or outlining my duties for the day. I am glad that she undertakes the cooking for I don't think I could match her efforts. Her pastries are incredible – no wonder her 'at homes' are so well-attended – and she is famous for the menus at the dinner parties she and Mr. Logan host.

The Logans have three children, two daughters and a son, and several grandchildren, all elsewhere. Mrs. Logan rues the distance between herself and her children and especially her grandchildren. However, she accommodates that in a good way, being kindness itself to other young people around her. In a few days she is holding a trousseau tea for a friend's daughter who is soon to be married. Mrs. Logan is accomplished at sewing but rather pushed for time now. She saw some of my needlework and asked me to finish some linen she was stitching for the bride-to-be, also some lingerie for her daughter in Vancouver. So I am as busy these days with my needle and thread as I am with the broom and dust cloth and I like it.

Finally, I must tell you about my lodgings. I wish you could see how I have moved up in the world – literally! I was content having my own room off the kitchen in Misty River. Here I have not one but three rooms to myself, and up on the second floor no less. There is my bedroom, a small but pleasant room with a high ceiling and a large window that lets in abundant sun. Next to it is my own bathroom, and beside that another small room with a sofa, a table and chair and a bookcase, a lovely place to relax. Being upstairs I have a grand view of the river valley to the front and the beautiful houses to the side and beyond.

Nice to be in a city again, with places to go on my day off – a public library, cinema, plenty of shops, even a church group on Sunday evenings for young men and women. I think I will like living in Edmonton.

Here I am going on and on about myself. I hope you don't mind – it's just that there has been so much happening. Odd isn't it, how life can drift along almost the same from day to day and week to week and it seems as if it will always be that way, and then something happens out of nowhere and everything is different before you have time to turn around. I would never have considered a fire a blessed event but I am tempted to do so now. As Grandma Sinclair used to say 'it's an ill wind that brings no good'. What is happening with you? Are you still liking your job at the newsagent's.? How is Ian – are you still seeing him? Do let me know how things are at home.

Much love,
Grace

A long letter, this one, I thought, as I wrote Phoebe's address on the envelope, stopping to make sure I had my own return address down right. I'll post it tomorrow when I go downtown on my afternoon off.

Only that wasn't quite how it happened, due to a telephone call early the next morning. I was in the kitchen doing up the breakfast dishes when Mrs. Logan came into the kitchen. "That was my friend Mrs. Sweeney who just called," Mrs. Logan said. "Her daughter Ruth is a public health nurse; I believe you met both of them at the 'at home' we had last week. Ruth is going out to make some calls today outside of the city and she has rather a lot to do. She wondered if you could go along with her to lend a hand. I think it would be good for you to get out and see a bit of the countryside around here and I'm sure you would find Ruth an interesting person to spend a day with. It's entirely up to you if you want to go. I know it's your afternoon off today but if you do choose to go along you can have tomorrow after-noon off instead."

I remembered Ruth; rather, Miss Sweeney, right away even though our meeting had been so brief we did not have the opportunity to say more than a few words to each other, what with so many people milling around. There was some-thing immensely likeable about the tall, sturdy, young woman; her friendly smile as she took a cup of tea and asked me how long I had been in the Logans' employ and how was I finding Edmonton. So instead of doing the usual mid-week round of household chores that morning and later taking the streetcar downtown for a bit of window shopping and a browse through the library, there I was, seated beside Miss Sweeney, absorbing her lively observations on the world around us as her weather-beaten vehicle forged its way west of the city.

"Just where are we going," I asked when the conversation slacked off for a moment.

"Oh, to the reserve," Miss McSweeney said. "Where native people live," she added, on seeing the questioning look on my face. "I guess you've never been to such a place before."

"No, no I haven't," I replied, shaking my head. "They are called Indians, are they not? I learned in school a long time ago how they ride on horseback with spears, hunting the buffalo on the plains. The mothers carried their babies – papooses, weren't they called? – on their backs in bags made out of deerskin that laced up the front, and the tribes moved around a lot."

"They used to, Grace. My goodness, you certainly paid attention in school, I must say," Miss McSweeney said with a hearty laugh. "Now they live on tracts of land called reserves, where they stay put and live in houses, some of them that is, for some still live in tents or teepees, although I wouldn't want to in this province in the wintertime, let me tell you. Some farm or raise cattle and horses, and others hunt and fish and live off the land that way. Anyway, the native people's health care falls under the federal government – for everyone else, the province is in charge – but the travelling nurses employed by the Department of Indian Affairs can't handle the workload alone; I think the department should hire more nurses, but that's not up to me. So the gist of it is that sometimes the department borrows district nurses like me who work for the province and gets us to do some of the work."

"And what is it you do on the reserves?" I asked.

"Well, I visit homes where someone is sick or injured, see how they're doing and if they need any help or advice. Sometimes I give talks at the clinic as well."

"And where would that be?"

"Oh in the community hall. A notice goes up on the bulletin board outside the room that's to be used for the clinic. Sometimes it's a well-baby clinic, sometimes there are short presentations on nutrition, sanitation, tips on homemaking, that sort of thing. In the spring, gardening is usually the topic of discussion as the women are encouraged to grow their own vegetables. Later in the season the talk turns to canning, putting their produce away for the winter. Today we're discussing health concerns in winter. That's where you come in."

"Just what is it I have to do?" I asked.

"Oh not to worry," she replied, taking in the uneasy look on my face. "You don't have to get up to the front and talk. Goodness knows I can do that well enough. You're going to help organize the display and keep track of things. Mrs. Anderson, one of the field matrons who works for the department, was supposed to help me but she's sick today. I was over at my mother's, fretting about what to do for a replacement, and my mother suggested Mrs. Logan might let you come along to help. We have a few other matters to attend to first, though. Ah here we are, almost at the reserve," Miss McSweeney said, slowing down the vehicle and turning off the main road.

"And here we are again," she said, pulling into a driveway in front of a white frame house. "Our first stop; let's see how the new mum and baby are doing." They were fine. Next stop was another white frame house where Miss McSweeney removed the sling from a young lad recovering from a broken collarbone and, after running her fingers along the trouble spot, pronounced the boy fit once more, urging him to be more careful. "Next time think twice before you jump down from the top rail on the fence, Jonathan." As we were leaving she eyed her patient's younger brother holding his hand with one finger sticking straight out. "And what have we here?" she asked, holding the youngster's hand to the window and rolling the swollen digit about. "I do believe there is a sliver in there that's troubling you." Fishing about in her bag, she located a small pick and a pair of tweezers and deftly removed the tiny piece of wood, then pushed to ease out the pus that had collected around it. "A soak in warm water and that finger will be fine," she said as she donned her coat, scarf and gloves and collected up her bag.

"Come along, Grace, we've got plenty yet to do today," she called out and we were off again.

"Next stop is where I put you to work. I need you to help me bring the display materials in from the car and set them up on a table towards the back of the room. Then while I'm talking at the front you can hand out the information sheets. Oh, and I want you to write down the names of the women who attend, so I can give a count to regional office."

Which is what I did, starting with the display, and once that was done Miss McSweeney took a leather-bound journal from her bag, turned to a fresh page, wrote the date and location across the top and handed her pen to me. "Sit down my dear and get ready... Here's your first customer," she said, waving at two women who had just come in. "Hello Hilda, good to see you. Is this your daughter? Come on over; my assistant will take your names down and then please go and find yourselves a seat."

The presentation drew quite the crowd, keeping me busy writing in the journal beforehand and handing out pamphlets afterwards. The afternoon flew by.

"Well, now that's done, we need to collect all this up, don't we?" Miss McSweeney said, motioning to the stack of towels and facecloths, the bars of soap and bottles of cough medicine and packages of cough drops we had placed on the table earlier. "Here, I'll take this lot out to the car and you pack up the rest, Grace. I'll be back in a minute," she said, picking up two boxes of rolled-up posters and heading outside.

I was so caught up with clearing the table that I didn't hear the door open again. "Need any help, miss?" a voice called out.

Startled, I gasped and looked up to see a young man garbed in the heavy dark parka and fur-trimmed hat of the RCMP.

"Remember me?" he asked, smiling as he reached out and caught a bottle of cough syrup before it rolled off the table.

"Oh, you're, you're the officer who was on duty the night of the fire in Misty River," I stammered.

"Yes, I was about to drive you to the young doctor's place when the good doctor himself appeared and deprived me of the opportunity. And I see you have a ride back to the city today with the public health nurse. All these people looking out for you, makes it hard for me to make your acquaintance."

"Well, uh," I said, trying to manage a laugh and only sounding flustered, hoping I wasn't turning red but fearing I was. "And what brings you here?" I asked, turning aside to put the jar in the box.

"Well, I was transferred not long after we happened to meet," he replied, sitting down on the edge of the table and unbuttoning his parka. "This is part of my new territory, you might say. I hear that you are employed in Edmonton now. I asked after you and Mrs. Robertson told me of your whereabouts, but she would not let on as to your address. Good thing I saw you going into the hall when you arrived today or I would have missed you altogether. By the way, my name is Peter, Peter Fergusson."

Just then the door opened and a familiar voice rang out. "Grace, do you have that last box ready? Oh, I didn't know you were in here, Constable Fergusson. I see that you have met my assistant," Miss McSweeney said, smiling just a little.

"Actually, we met some time ago, back in the winter and we're just getting reacquainted," he replied.

"Well, you will have to continue that later," Miss McSweeney said, firmly but still smiling. "Grace and I have another stop to make before we go back to the city, and it's getting late."

The constable smiled back. "Goodness, I wouldn't want to keep you. Here, let me take the box out to your vehicle," he said, picking it up before either of us had a chance to say anything. After he stowed the box away and shut the trunk lid he took off his hat and bowed slightly. "See you again," he said, before putting his hat back on and striding off towards the band office.

"We're going to see how Mrs. Arcand is coming along," Miss McSweeney said as she started the car. "She's had a lot of trouble with her ankle, a pesky ulcer that refuses to go away. I lanced it last time I was out here but it may require more treatment. I didn't like the look of it. She lives just over yonder; it won't take long for us to swing by and see how she is doing."

The car bumped along, until Miss McSweeney broke the silence. "Looks like you have an admirer," she teased me as we made our way to our next stop.

"Oh, not at all," I laughed, flustered, trying not to blush. "He was just saying hello. We met some time ago, actually we met after the fire in Misty River. He was one of the officers sent to the scene."

"I know all about it, Grace," Miss M. said with a twinkle in her eye. "Constable Fergusson filled me in on the details when I went back to the vehicle to get the rest of my things before the presentation this afternoon. You were in the hall getting ready. I suggested he drop by later. Don't worry, he's a good sort. I've known him for a while now." Turning briefly towards me she smiled and said, "I even took the liberty of letting him know where you live."

"You didn't!' I exclaimed. "I… I…."

"Yes, I did," Miss M. said. "What is so horrible about that? He's a nice young man; after all, his family's from Scotland so he must be all right. His parents came over here the year before he was born. So now you'll have something to talk about when he comes calling."

She slowed down. "And here we are at Mrs. Arcand's house," she said, turning the car into a short driveway alongside another frame house, this one painted light blue. "Oh hello, Iris, is your grandmother home?" Miss McSweeney called out to the young woman who greeted us as we approached the front step. "I was out here for a gathering at the community hall and I figured I should check that sore on your grandmother's ankle. This is Grace Sinclair, who came along today to help me out. Grace, this is Iris Arcand."

I said hello to the young woman, who smiled shyly and grasped my extended hand. "Come in, my grandmother is sitting out in the kitchen having a cup of tea. Would you like some?" she asked us.

"Well I won't say no to that," Miss McSweeney said, bending down to take off her boots. "It's been a hectic day for the both of us, hasn't it Grace?"

Before I had time to say anything, a woman's voice called out, "Is that you, Miss McSweeney? Come in, come in."

As soon as we pulled off our boots Iris led us down a brief hall to the kitchen, where I saw an elderly woman sitting in the corner by the stove. "I thought I recognized that voice," the woman said, her face breaking into a smile as she eased herself out of the rocking chair, knocking two patchwork cushions from the seat onto the floor. "Come and have a chair at the table," she said, limping slightly as she shuffled across the room. "Iris, bring some cups and saucers for our guests, and those biscuits from the counter. You picked a good day to drop in; I baked this morning," she said.

After setting the tea things in place, along with the plate of biscuits, a butter dish and a small pot of jam, she pulled a chair close to the table and sat herself down, groaning ever so slightly.

"My ankle still hurts. Would you have a look at it when we're done?" she asked Miss McSweeney, who replied, "I certainly will."

A pleasant half hour or so passed, with several cups of tea poured and the plate of biscuits passed around two, if not three, times, conversation flowing all the while: how Mrs. Arcand's garden had been good this year; how the raspberries and saskatoons were thick along the river, which meant a lot of time in the kitchen making jam but it was worth it; how the men were doing well on their hunting and fishing trips, how Miss McSweeney liked being detailed to the reserve and other points outside Edmonton which aroused much curiosity from her colleagues stuck in the city.

Suddenly Mrs. Arcand bent over and rolled down her sock, prompting Miss McSweeney to set her cup down, push her chair over and pull her bag up to her lap. "Go get me another pair of socks, Iris, and take your friend with you," the older woman said, motioning towards the bedrooms beyond the kitchen.

Iris led the way to her grandmother's bedroom, where, once inside, she whispered to me. "Grandma doesn't like other people around when the nurse is looking at her," she said, shrugging her shoulders and smiling. "That's just the way she is."

I smiled. "I understand." While Iris rooted around in one of the drawers of her grandmother's dresser, I surveyed the objects scattered here and there on top of the dresser. A comb and brush set with a hand mirror, a brooch, and a few hair ribbons.

"Oh here's a good pair," Iris said, pulling two grey woollen socks out of the drawer. "Grandma likes these ones; let's go and give them to her." As I followed Iris out of the room, something on top of the dresser caught my eye, a small leather pouch adorned with dark pink and red beadwork. That looks familiar, I thought. Now where have I seen that before?

That question niggled at me the rest of the day, consuming my thoughts so thoroughly I could concentrate on nothing else. "You're awfully quiet, what's on your mind?" Miss McSweeney asked as we made their way back to the city. "Still thinking about the young constable?"

"Oh you, will you stop that," I said, flustered once more. "It's nothing, I'm just a wee bit tired." But the unanswered question wouldn't let go, coming back to me as I cleaned up after the evening meal that night and again the next day as I rode the bus downtown on my postponed afternoon off. Indeed, it got to the point every time I thought about that afternoon at the settlement I found myself pondering the beaded pouch on top of the grandmother's dresser, wondering why it looked familiar. Where had I seen it before?

Chapter Fifteen

"Well I must say, you made quite an impression on your trip to the countryside," Mrs. Logan said the next afternoon as I stepped into the kitchen after sweeping out the back pantry. "That was Mrs. McSweeney on the telephone, and just about all she had to talk about was how helpful you were and how much Ruth enjoyed your company. I'll have to watch that I don't lose you to the McSweeneys," she chuckled as she sat down at her desk in the corner to write the grocery list. "I know we need cinnamon; are there any other spices we're running low on, Grace?"

"Nutmeg for sure, and let me check, I think we're just about out of allspice as well," I replied as I opened a cupboard door and looked over the spice rack attached to the back of the door. "Yes, we're short on both, and basil and sage for that matter. By the way, I rather enjoyed the outing yesterday, Mrs. Logan. I wouldn't be averse to doing it again."

Edmonton, Alberta,
December 22, 1924.

Dear Phoebe,

Your letter was such a happy one, a real joy to read. I am so glad you are enjoying your work and that everyone is well. I too am liking my work for the most part. There is always something going on around here – someone coming over for tea and a chat with Mrs. Logan or several ladies for a meeting in the front parlour, or a few of Mr. Logan's friends returning books and staying a while to talk. Many a Saturday evening the Logans host one of their famous dinner parties, with nine or ten courses no less, so plenty to do helping Mrs. Logan turn out all that's listed on the menu, setting the dining room table and then serving the fine meal. That is a bit nerve-wracking for me – I am always afraid I will trip and splash soup on one of the guests or drop the tray when I bring the cups and saucers in for tea and coffee. Nothing disastrous has happened so far, thank heavens.

A few weeks ago I was busy helping Mrs. Logan get ready for Christmas, putting up the tree in the parlour, hanging wreaths on the front and back doors and tying evergreen boughs on the staircase railing. The Logans love to entertain any time of the year and especially at Christmas, which means more kitchen and dining room duty. But I've been able to get out and look at the lights downtown. I hope the gift I sent you has arrived. I received your package last week – thank you very much – and will open it Christmas morning.

I had the most interesting experience recently. I went to a native settlement, or reserve as they are usually called. (You remember we learned about them briefly in geography, when we were studying North America.) Mrs. Logan has a friend whose daughter is a public health nurse, actually a district nurse for the province. She travels around rural areas dealing with a range of health concerns, seeing patients in towns, villages and on farms. Sometimes she is asked to fill in on the reserves as well.

The friend's daughter, Miss McSweeney, was giving a presentation at a reserve near Edmonton and the woman who was going to help her was ill the day they were scheduled to go so I was asked to fill in.

When we reached the reserve we called in on a few patients at their homes and then went to the community hall for the presentation which was about health concerns in winter. My job was to help put up a display, look after the attendance sheet and hand out information booklets. That went fine. Afterwards, when I was helping Miss McSweeney pack up, who turned up but the RCMP constable I saw at the night of the fire in Misty River. He offered to help me and I asked him to take me to take me to Dr. and Mrs. Robertson's place but Dr. Robertson appeared so I never did learn the constable's name or anything about him. Apparently he asked after me later but by that time I had moved to Edmonton and Mrs. Robertson, not knowing the young man, was reluctant to let on my whereabouts. Miss McSweeney does know him so when he saw me going into the hall she was only too happy to answer his questions. I spoke to him for just a few minutes, long enough to find out his name is Peter Fergusson and he is pleasant enough. Miss McSweeney told me more about him on the way back to the city, that his parents came to Alberta from Scotland, his father was also on the force, back when it was called the North-West Mounted Police, and his parents live in Edmonton 'so maybe he will call on you next time he is back for a visit with his family,' she said. Well we shall see about that.

As if there hadn't been enough activity in the day, we finished the afternoon stopping at another patient's home on the reserve, an older woman who had a very nice granddaughter staying with her. After Miss McSweeney saw to the ulcer on the grandmother's leg we all had tea and biscuits together. I enjoyed the day and I hope Miss McSweeney asks me to go again.

I'm afraid I must go. It's my afternoon off and I'm meeting a girl who works at the house two doors down. She's from England and came over a few months before I did. I met her at our church youth group last Sunday evening. Merry Christmas to you and yours.

Love to all,
Grace

"You went *there*... to see those dirty savages? How could you? Weren't you afraid they would tie you down and scalp you or something?" asked Margaret from two doors down as the trolley rumbled along the avenue.

"No I wasn't," I said. "And they aren't dirty and they aren't savages. Where did you get such ideas? Have you ever met a native person?"

"No, but that's what everyone says they are."

"Then everyone's wrong."

Chapter Sixteen

"So here we are again," Miss McSweeney said with a hearty laugh as she parked the car abruptly in front of the community hall at the settlement. "Oh look at you, you've got everything so neatly arranged there," she said, gazing over the record book and a cluster of pens bundled together in the leather satchel sitting on my lap. "Sometimes I think you're too organized for your own good, my dear. You just watch, I'll have you out here more times than you care for, at the rate you're going."

"I don't think I'd mind," I replied, smiling as I opened the car door.

"You might think otherwise when the snow is knee-high and you have to get out and push when we get stuck. We haven't had much snow so far this winter but there is bound to be a lot more ahead," she said as she followed me up the stairs leading to the hall. "And who do we have here?"

It was Iris, standing inside the vestibule, leaning against the entrance door to the main hall. The young woman's eyes lit up when she saw the two of us.

"Well, well, Iris, what can I do for you today? Is your grand-mother's ankle acting up again?"

Iris hesitated ever so slightly. "It hasn't really healed, Miss McSweeney. I was wondering if you could come and take a look at it. Grandma makes light of it but I think it bothers her a lot some days."

"That I can do, my dear. We'll be over just as soon as the presentation is over," Miss McSweeney said, sweeping into the hall, intent on setting up for another busy afternoon.

As I followed behind her I turned just before we went through the main door and called back to Iris, who was departing the vestibule and about to head down the front steps. "I was hoping you'd be here. I'll see you later," I said, and both of us smiled.

There followed an industrious afternoon, the topic being sanitation and how to keep the risk of tuberculosis at bay in the midst of winter with everyone cooped up inside at close range. So many people turned out I could hardly keep up listing the names but managed somehow, grateful when the presentation began so I could sit down. The pace picked up again once the presentation was over, there being several pamphlets to give out to each person leaving the hall.

"Need any help miss?" a vaguely familiar voice asked as I scouted around under the table for a box to put the remaining pamphlets in.

"Oh, it's you again,' I said, looking up at the smiling constable standing beside me.

"Yes, it's me, and I can get that for you," he said, reaching down and whisking the box out from under the table. "I tried to reach you last time I was in the city. I called at your home but no one was there. Must have been your afternoon off and you were out and about."

Chapter Seventeen

Edmonton, Alberta,
February 7, 1925

Dear Phoebe,

So good to hear from you as always. Sounds like you had a busy Christmas, with all the family gathering at your house. I am glad you like the pincushion I made you for Christmas. Thank you very much for the stationary you sent me. The flowers you tatted on the corner of each sheet of paper are so pretty.

Christmas was hectic here as well. One of the Logans' daughters was here from Vancouver with her husband and two young children, and there were many other visitors dropping in. I poured countless cups of tea and carried in plate upon plate of shortbread and Christmas cake. For Christmas dinner there were sixteen people around the table in the dining room. It was at four o'clock and after that I finished the washing up I was able to get away to a Christmas dinner put on at church for the young people working away from home. I enjoyed myself but, of course, suffered the usual attack of homesickness that accompanies any special occasion.

It seems to me I promised last letter to tell you more about my visit to the native settlement. I've actually been back there once more and would you believe I ran into the RCMP officer I told you about, the constable *who attended the fire in Misty River and who I saw on my first trip to the reserve. The week after I saw him the second time on the reserve I received a letter from him to say he was going to be in Edmonton for a training course and would call on me the following Sunday afternoon.*

Which he did. We went for a walk down the avenue and then we had tea in the kitchen – Mrs. Logan said that would be fine and she came in to say hello to Peter. She hadn't met him before but she knows some of his family, a cousin and her husband, I think it is; anyway they live here in Edmonton. Miss McSweeney's mother knows them as well. He has finished the course and has returned to his post outside the city. I am seeing him again next week when we both get some extra time off for working over Christmas. I don't know where we will go this time but I am looking forward to it. He is interesting and well-mannered and has a good sense of humour. I think I rather like him.

Oh and I meant to tell you more about the native lady and her granddaughter Miss McSweeney and I went to see at the settlement. This was a new experience for me. Actually, attending the presentation was new enough – I had never been in contact with native people before. Remember the school books – how the natives were called savages and redskins. Such a negative portrayal and not true at all. For one thing, they have brown skin, and everyone I met was nice to me. Anyway, we went to see Mrs. Arcand, who is diabetic and has trouble with a stubborn ulcer on her leg. Her granddaughter, Iris, was there. Iris is a pleasant girl, quiet at first but once you get to know her she livens up. Indeed, she reminds me of you. I enjoyed every minute I spent with them, relaxing in the kitchen over a cup of tea, munching on biscuits, chatting about the weather and what's going on at the settlement. For the first time since leaving Inverness I felt completely at home, so comfortable and at ease – something I didn't realize I was missing until that afternoon at Mrs. Arcand's house. To be fair, I don't think that could have happened at Diamond Coulee in light of the circumstances – Robert was still burdened with grief over Elizabeth when I arrived and then so guilt-stricken when Rosemary thrust herself into our lives, and in Misty River, well, I have made it clear to you before what that was like.

My current situation is a thousand times better but even so, I'm still the domestic, the live-in help who works for the homeowners. I don't mean to sound ungrateful to the Logans; they are lovely people and you couldn't ask for better employers. It's just that at Mrs. Arcand's house I'm Grace Sinclair, the young woman from Scotland who lives in Edmonton and comes to the settlement with Miss McSweeney.

Speaking of Robert, I heard from him not long ago. When I reached Edmonton I sent him a brief note informing him of my move and my new address. He tells me he is enjoying his work as principal at Irvine, the school is gaining students and my nieces are doing well, also that the new baby, a boy, has arrived, a bit early but he is healthy nonetheless. Well at least they let me know. I suppose I should get something to send the wee one, I'll see. I still miss Alice and Louisa. I wonder if they remember me at all, just as I wonder if people in Inverness ever think of me, besides you of course. I've been away for a while, that's all.

Please say hello to for me to the woman at the newsagent's and my best to Ian.

All my love,
Grace

Chapter Eighteen

"I told you that you would get this job if you didn't watch out," Miss McSweeney said with a laugh as the vehicle lurched way along the road leading to the settlement. "Looks like it's yours."

"I don't mind a bit," Grace said. "Tell me one thing, if there's not to be a presentation what do we have to do that takes up the entire afternoon and you need me along to help."

The familiar smile reappeared as Miss McSweeney began talking. "I just thought it would be nice for you to get out and see Iris again," she said, looking over in my direction briefly before turning her attention back to the road. "You two seem to have struck up quite a friendship, and I know if we don't go to her you won't get to see her. It's not as if she's about to show up on your doorstep, the way the young constable does, that is," she teased me. Then, sounding more serious, she went on. "I know from talking to the domestics my mother and her friends have had over the years that isolation is the worst part of the job. There are people all around but no one to chum with really, except maybe at a church group or at the tea room on your afternoon off. When I see how you and Iris get along I want to encourage it, that's all.

"Oh here we are at our first stop," she said, pulling into the lane behind a house I had not visited before. "We'll see how

89

the new baby is doing here, then we have Mrs. Cardinal over there – she's just home from the hospital in Edmonton, and I need to see how she's getting along. And then we can stop in for a look at Mrs. Arcand's leg and a visit with her and Iris. How does that sound?"

Three cups of tea and two scones later I sat back, motioning 'no thank-you' as the tea pot hovered above my cup and saucer. "I'll float home at this rate," I told Mrs. Arcand, who put the pot back on the wood stove and sat herself down, picking up her needlework as she did so. "Iris, I need that bag of embroidery thread – I think it's on my dresser but I'm not sure. Would you go to my bedroom and look for it for me? And take Grace with you. No sense in leaving her here."

Down the hall we went and looked about for the bag of thread which was not to be found, at least not right away. A thorough search of the cluttered dresser top proved fruitless. "Granny has so much stuff here," Iris said as she sifted through a heap of greeting cards and letters.

"Here, you start there," she said, motioning to the far end of the dresser, "and I'll start at this end and we'll see what we can find."

"Maybe in the mending basket?" Iris murmured softly to herself, pulling through a heap of socks and bits of wool. "No, not there," she said, turning her attention to an enormous pin cushion flanked by spools of thread.

After watching Iris for a bit, I tucked into the task, shuffling aside a china dog and a jar of buttons to get at a stack of leaflets of some kind or other. There seemed to be something underneath the printed material. I lifted up the papers and there it was again, the beaded leather pouch. "I've seen this somewhere before, I'm sure of it," I said, picking up the pouch and holding it out to Iris. "I can't quite place it. Just a minute, I know... My Grandfather Sinclair had one just like it. It was on the dresser in the bedroom upstairs ever since I can remember. It stayed there even after he died. Grandma kept it. I asked Grandpa one time about it, where it was from and he just said he got it when he was in Canada working for the Hudson Bay Company. I wanted to know more about it, who made it and how it was done, but Grandpa said he couldn't recall and that was that," I said, cupping the pouch in one hand and running the fingers of my other hand over the beaded flower pattern.

Glancing up, I saw that Iris was looking straight at me, a puzzled look on her face. "So you had family over here, a long time ago, I mean?" Iris asked, moving towards me until the two of us were shoulder to shoulder, both of us staring down at the leather pouch in my hand.

And then it all came out, how a few months before Iris had overhead her grandmother and another older woman from the settlement talking about the Orkneymen they had known many years before, men who had signed up with the Hudson Bay Company to make boats – 'York boats' they called them – for the fur traders, and once their time was up with the company the men who made the boats in the workshop at Fort Edmonton went away, returning to their distant homeland across the sea. "I couldn't hear everything Granny and her friend said, they were speaking so softly. I was really curious about it all but I couldn't bring it up because Granny and her friend thought they were alone. Not long after, one of the girls at school talked about country wives, when the white men took native women as wives, but I don't think they always got married in church. They were just sort of married I guess. I asked Granny about that but she avoided my question. She changed the subject and I knew not to ask again.

"There's something else I think I'm not supposed to know about. Not long after that day I was here with Granny when she was looking for something in her top drawer and an old picture fell down out onto the floor. Granny picked it up in a flash and put it right back in the drawer. I sneaked in later and found it hidden under her handkerchiefs. Here, let's see if I can find it again," Iris said.

First, she went to the bedroom door and stuck her head out into the hallway. "They're still talking, we're safe." Then she went over to her grandmother's dresser. Carefully, slowly, she pulled the top drawer of the dresser open. "It's a photograph of a man, and the minute I laid eyes on it I saw a likeness between him and my mother."

Iris rooted around in the back corner of the drawer for a minute or two. "Here, here it is," she whispered triumphantly, pulling out a small black and white photograph, its edges curled and yellow. I crept up to Iris and looked over her shoulder.

"May I have a closer look?" I asked.

"Of course," Iris said, handing over the image of a bearded young man.

"Can it be?" I murmured to myself, my heart thudding.

"I didn't dare say anything but I figured it out. He was my grandfather," Iris said, her voice hushed, excited.

"And mine as well," I responded, as we crushed each other in our arms.

The End

Epilogue

Edmonton
January 1995

I am old now. Where the years went I don't know, just that they
flew by and here I am, sorting through things, getting ready to
leave my home of forty-plus years and move into seniors' hous-
ing. Not a lodge, my daughters are quick to point out. Assisted
living, it is called. Actually, the new place looks quite nice. I
expect it will take some getting used to, going from a spacious
two-storey house to a three-room suite, but I can handle it.

I'm knee deep in boxes upon boxes of picture albums, letters and other bits of this and that amassed over time. My children and their children have asked for pictures from my youth
and I'm happy to oblige. I can't take all of this with me. I've
put one box aside for my special things – our wedding picture –
Peter in his dress uniform, me in the linen suit I sewed myself –
and a few photos each of son Jonathon and daughters Lucy
and Emma, and the picture Phoebe sent from her wedding day.
Dear Phoebe, gone so long now. What a shock it was that summer day more than fifty years ago, opening up the letter from
her daughter, telling me of her mother's sudden death.

Losing my closest friend from home devastated me. Even
now, decades later, through the phases of marriage, mother-
hood and beyond, I feel the loss keenly. Maybe that is why I
never went back to Inverness. Goodness knows Peter suggested
it often enough, every time he was promoted and there was
more money coming in, but I always put him off. There would
be a graduation or wedding coming, or another grandchild on

the way, some occasion or other to keep me nearby. Maybe the real reason was that the people I most wanted to see were gone.

Not that I didn't keep in touch, far from it. My daughters teased me that I kept the postal service in business. I still hear from Simon's family, Phoebe's daughter as well. And yes, Robert's girls do remember me, even come to see me now and then.

And what of Iris you may wonder. For the first few years the bond we shared was our secret, much cherished. We considered letting on that we knew who the man in the picture was but we didn't want to upset Iris's grandmother whom we both loved so much. After she died we saw no reason to hide our connection. The relatives in Scotland who would have been most rattled were long gone and, anyway, so what if anyone was bothered. I was proud of my link to the first people of my adopted country and I still am.

We saw each other as often as we could and kept in touch between visits – no small challenge considering how often Peter was transferred. I was so happy Edmonton was his final posting; it meant I could see Iris more often and her children and mine could know one another. When she died three years ago the darkness that settled in a corner of my heart when Phoebe passed on, widened, almost overwhelming me on some days.

Yet all is not lost. Our families are still close. Last summer one of Iris's granddaughters and one of mine journeyed to Orkney, hiking through the windblown isles that brought them together. The young women returned with many photographs, one of which they had enlarged and framed for me. This striking image of the harbour at Stromness, where my grandfather boarded the HBC ship that brought him to Canada, is packed amongst my treasures in the special box, ready to go with me to my new home.

Acknowledgements

The following people are much appreciated for their help in making this book happen: the late Helen Boyko, the staff (past and present) at Rutherford House, Jane Ross and the Battle River Writers' Group, and of course my family.